The Story Collectc

Illusions
of the
Mist

E.S. Barrison

Illusions of the Mist/E.S. Barrison. -- 1st ed.
ISBN 979-8-9853634-2-5

DEDICATED TO GRANDMA RHODA & GRANDPA
DAVID

THESE CHARACTER, THIS SERIES, IT'S ALL FOR
YOU.

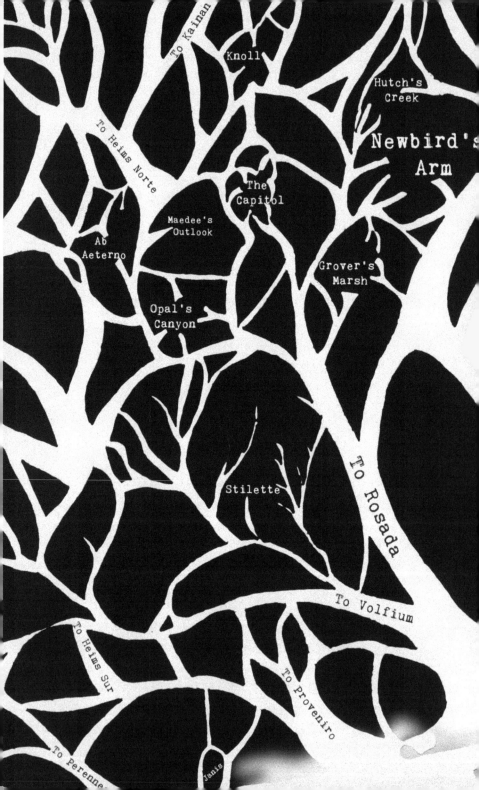

The Council of Mist Keepers

NINGURSU
The God of Death

AELIA
The Healer

TOMAS
The Peacemaker

JULIETTA
The Painter

JIANG
Null

MALAIKA
The Cartographer

ALOJZY
The Architect

CAROLINE
The Illusionist

BRENT
The Story Collector

AL•MA•NAC

a publication containing astronomical or meteorological information, as future positions of celestial objects, star magnitudes, and culmination dates of constellations.

FOREWARD

S tories. That's what everything has always been.
That's what it always shall be.

They say to understand who we are, who we shall be, we need to understand our tales.

I understand that more than anyone.

Shortly before my twenty-first birthday, I met a mysterious woman in black: Caroline Elisabeth Walsh, the Eighth Member of the Council of Mist Keepers, affectionally known as the Illusionist. She told me a truth that nearly broke me: I would join the Council of Mist Keepers, the Gods of Death, and give up the life I'd always known.

But I'm not here to tell my story.

It feels as though an eternity has passed since I first learned of the Council of Mist Keepers. Perhaps that is because the mist has granted me the ability to see stories and understand the past. My head hurts every day, and I question who I am when I'm swarmed by the voices of other people.

But I ground myself with these stories and remind myself that the Council of Mist Keepers is merely a group of humans. They are not as powerful as the stars. They're human, just like me. It is my job to understand their past, their present, and their future. Perhaps then I can protect those I love and those to come.

I've made it my duty to record their stories, starting with my former teacher, Caroline Walsh. Because no matter where I go, where I run, or how many stories fill my head, I know one truth.

I am the Story Collector.

And you cannot hide your story from me.

- *Brenton Rob Harley*
Ninth Member of the Council of Mist Keepers
The Story Collector

ONE

The sky turned green during the Night of Firefraught Lights. Once a year, the entire town of Arfiskeby gathered on the pier to watch the lights dance while welcoming the grip of winter. They danced beneath the stars, enamored by carnival games and peculiar masks, while singing songs to their goddess, the Constable Gelida.

Everyone celebrated.

Well, everyone except for Caroline.

Rather than join the festivities on the pier, Caroline ventured to a secluded cliff on the east side of town, where not a single fire burned. Neither her sister nor brother wanted to join her, and that was fine by her. Caroline savored the dark, letting it gather over her body. Her father wouldn't be happy that she went to the cliff alone, but she didn't care.

Every day, she ventured to this clifftop, waiting for the fishing boat carrying her mother to return. Her mother promised that they would return on the Night of Firefraught Lights after a month of sailing and harvesting fish from past the permafrost. They called the land beyond the permafrost the Helvidim, where the Constable Gelida sent all those who did her wrong. At night, Caroline prayed the Constable would be kind to her mother, and they might return with a wealth of fish to feed the town.

She unraveled the fishing net she kept behind the rocks, combing out the knots before casting out into the water. *In one year, I shall get to go out to sea with you, Mama.* Caroline smiled as the net floated into the water. It had been an obsession of hers for years: she would join her mother on the boat, and as a team, they would catch fish for the town.

One year. She could count the number of days now.

One year.

For now, Caroline gripped the rope and waited for whatever fish the Constable blessed her with that day. Some said on the Night of Firefraught Lights, the largest fish came out to play. Perhaps if she caught one, they'd allow her onto the boats early.

The elders of the village said only those who had sur-passed their thirteenth year could go on the boats. Her older sister, Victoria, had that privilege, though she despised the way the water rocked the boats. Caroline yearned for that opportunity, though, ever since she first snuck onto a boat at the ripe age of eight years old. Her mother discovered as they neared the permafrost, forcing the boat to turn around and return her home. The lecture that followed still occupied Caroline's mind as she lowered the net into the water.

"Caroline," her mother scolded, "I have told you once, and I shall say it again: the Constable cannot save children from the bites of frost. If you were to fall into her consarn arms, she would send you home on the arms of a snowflake...but you would no longer be you. You would be a drop of snow. We cannot lose you to the Constable's arms. So, I implore you to stay here, my child, until your thirteenth year comes alas."

It was a dramatic speech, but Caroline held her mother's words close. While she didn't believe most of the preacher's sermons, she still quivered beneath the Constable's gaze. The Constable's existence remained an unarguable fact, as every morning, the fog rose over the sea, warning Caroline of the horrors on the waves.

Perhaps her sister was right to stay away from the sea. But Caroline longed for the adventure, the one that her mother took by boat each day. Her mother always returned, no matter the weather or the density of the Constable's fog. Caroline believed her mother to be more powerful than even the Constable.

To Caroline, her mother commanded the sea.

She tugged at her net and scowled in disappointment. *Once again, not a single bite.* The lights from the festival shimmered in the distance. Cheers echoed. *They are most likely scaring off the fish.*

After a few more rounds of casting out the net with naught a fish to show for her trouble, Caroline refolded her net and started her descent down the cliffside. She eyed the sea one last time. Not a single boat graced the horizons, only the fragile mist of the permafrost.

Mama should have arrived on the horizon by now. Where is she? Caroline glanced at the net in her arms. Perhaps she could impress her mother before the boats returned.

Caroline hopped upon a rock at the bottom of the cliff, ignoring the waves that thrashed against her shoes, and cast out her net again. She held her breath, waiting for any signs of fish or life.

She could only pray for the Constable's help as the Firefraught Lights reined above her. They glimmered in response to her prayer, and in the distance, another cheer roared from the festival in the distance along with the final utterance.

The net thrashed.

Caroline whooped to herself, then wrung her hands through the net. She laced the rope around her hands thrice and positioned herself on the rocks. With a grunt, she tugged on the net.

It didn't budge.

"What in the Constable's name is happening?" Caroline asked. She positioned herself again and once more tugged on the net.

Nothing.

She cursed the Constable under her breath, then tried one last thing. She wrapped the edge of the net around her entire body, then, with her whole weight, she ran back toward the path, dragging the net behind her.

Whatever she caught thrashed about, trying its best to escape. Caroline didn't dare look, only listening as what had been trapped dragged onto the shore, then hit the rocks.

She heaved and collapsed against the rocks. Her heart raced. Did she dare look at what she caught? *Mama does not fear her fish. Neither should I.*

Caroline slowly turned her head towards the shoreline.

A shimmering fish the size of a man lay on the rock, its gills opening and closing, mouth ajar. Its silver eyes stared at her without blinking.

Caroline backed away and screamed, "Papa! Papa! I need to show you something! Papa!"

TWO

Caroline found her father, brother, and sister down by the pier celebrating the Night of Firefraught lights. Masked patrons threw fire in the air, painting the sky in an array of colors while dancers spun amid the multicolored snow. Caroline pushed past them all, tugging on her father's hand and leading him with her siblings to where she caught the fish. She gripped him tight, wrapping her small hand around the ruby bejeweled ring on his finger.

The moment her father saw the tremendous silver fish, he released Caroline and ran off to the pier again. Her siblings, Victoria and William, gawked at the beast. No one spoke, each of them taking a moment to pray for the soul of the fish as it traveled into the arms of the Constable Gelida, as per tradition. Usually, it was a solemn moment, but Caroline couldn't refrain from the excitement budding in her chest.

I caught the biggest fish I've ever seen! I can't believe it!

Her father returned with the mayor of Arfiskeby and the well-regarded Priestess Abernathy about an hour later. An entourage from the festival followed close behind them, still decorated in animal masks.

Caroline raced to her father's side, once again wrapping her hand around his ruby-ringed fingers. The priestess knelt beside the fish and pressed her fingers above its eye, then smiled. "It is a coruscaish."

"Is that not a legend?" the mayor asked.

Caroline peeked past her father at the fish. *A coruscaish.* Her mother once told her of these fish. The story said that the Constable Gelida rode on the back of glistening fish on summer days. She called them the coruscaish for their glistening skin and silver eyes.

"Do not deny what the Constable has given us. It is our blessing for the year." Priestess Abernathy rose. "We shall feast on the coruscaish, and it will grant us prosperity for years to come!"

The crowd cheered.

Priestess Abernathy turned towards Caroline. "And to begin this wonderful feast, on this glorious Night of Firefraught Lights, it is tradition that the one who caught the coruscaish will make the first cut." She removed a dull fishing blade from her long robe and handed it to Caroline. "Go along, angel."

"Right now?" Caroline asked as she took the blade.

"Yes. We must sacrifice any large fish at once, so its soul may return to the Constable Gelida again." Her father nudged her. "Go on, dear. It is your first catch."

Caroline glanced at him, taking in the kindness in his blue eyes, then glanced at her siblings. Victoria stood with her arms crossed, glowering at the fish, while William gazed in utter amazement. He smiled at Caroline.

"Okay." Caroline turned back to the fish and approached it. Her fingers trembled as she raised the blade over the fish's stomach.

Then she jabbed the knife into its body.

Silver blood pooled from the fish's body. The crowd whooped again.

Caroline watched the blood beneath the Firefraught Lights. The stream of silver dripped off the rocks and into the ocean. As more and more pooled out, it turned red.

Priestess Abernathy rushed to Caroline's side. She gasped, took the knife from Caroline, and leaned over the fish.

Caroline watched in horror as the woman peeled back the fish's skin. The scent of rotting meat filled the air.

Restraining the urge to vomit, Caroline focused on one of her mother's lessons. *I know the fish smells bad, Caroline. Instead, focus on your favorite smell. Keep it right there...then you won't smell it anymore. That is your essence.*

She inhaled a few times, recalling the way the waves rolled across the sea, and the scent vanished.

But the sight did not.

The priestess remained hunched over the fish, hands trembling as she spoke, "Oh for sard's sake, Constable. Not tonight."

The mayor approached. "Mam, what is it?"

The priestess reached into the fish's body and removed an object.

Caroline's stomach dropped. Her entire world spun at the mere sight.

The priestess held a human arm.

And upon the hand sat a ruby-encrusted ring that belonged to Caroline's mother.

THREE

The entire town came together to mourn Caroline's mother. They built a funeral pyre for the dismembered arm and sent it out to sea, mourning the late Katherine Walsh. Caroline stood there without tears, holding her brother William's hand as he sobbed, and her sister bowed her head in dismay. Their father hadn't said a word since they found the arm. He slept most of the days and spent his nights wandering the streets. When home, he did not dare look Caroline in the eye.

Really, the entire town looked at her differently. People shied away from her as she walked in the street, and one man went as far to spit in her face. But she kept her head high. It wasn't her fault that the corucaish ate her mother.

Mama can't be dead, she reminded herself. The Constable Gelida wouldn't be that cruel.

As the funeral pyre floated out to sea, Priestess Abernathy chanted, "So it says the corucaish are the sole steeds of the Constable. If they have indeed eaten one of our own, a dark time is upon us. Today, we mourn Katherine Walsh, but tomorrow, we prepare. We shall not sit idly by and wait for our death."

"But what of the girl who found the corucaish?" someone shouted.

Caroline raised her eyebrow. Why should they blame her for the corucaish's actions? She merely caught the beast. Should they not celebrate her discovery? She found the bad omen before it snuck upon them.

"Yes! She found the beast! She must be punished!" another person added.

"We can have the lead blocks ready by morning and drown her before the curse of the corucaish takes shape!" a third person remarked.

"Now, now!" Priestess Abernathy held up her hands. "I believe the child has suffered enough. She has lost her mother to this beast, after all. It is not her fault the beast made its appearance."

Caroline clenched William's hand tighter. *But Mama isn't gone. I'll find her.*

The priestess's words quelled the uproar. They finished the ceremony in silence, watching as the pyre glimmered against the dark daytime sky. Once the pyre vanished on the horizon, Priestess Abernathy pressed her lips to a ram's horn and blew a final goodbye to the deceased.

Caroline stood at the edge of the water with her family as the townsfolk took their leave. No one spoke, the heaviness like a cloak on their backs. Her father left the shoreline first, with Victoria on his heels, trying her best to comfort him. Caroline stayed, still holding William's hand.

Mama can't be gone. Her mother was one of the greatest fishers in Arfiskeby. Perhaps the best in the entire nation of Heims!

She couldn't have fallen off her ship.

She wouldn't have let a fish eat her.

"What are we going to do without Mummy, Caroline?" William sniffled.

Caroline glanced at her brother. She placed an awkward arm around his shoulders. "I do not think she is gone."

"But the priestess said—"

"I refuse to believe she is gone. Will, I promise, I will find her."

"How?"

"I will sail out to sea, I will hunt every fish, and I will slaughter every monster until I find her."

"You are going to be a fisher like Mummy?"

"I will not just be a fisher." Caroline smiled at her brother. "I will be the best one ever."

FOUR

The day after her mother's funeral, Caroline took her net to the same place where she'd caught the corucaish. A few townsfolk tossed glares her way as she walked, but she kept her head high. It didn't matter to her what they thought; she would become the best, even if it took years.

At the edge of the cliff, she tossed out her net and waited. She waited for hours, counting the blessings in the stars while twiddling her thumbs. When she reeled in the net at high noon, not a single fish graced her presence.

She adjusted her position and tried again.

And again.

This went on for three weeks. In the shadow of night, the water flowed like blood, but when the moon glowed, or the Firefraught Lights shimmered, the water appeared silver. Caroline cast her net into it with a prayer to the Constable Gelida on her lips.

Then she waited.

She spent those moments enamored with her memories. Her mother used to sit with her on the pier, showing her different baits, all while telling stories about the Constable. Before Caroline ever wanted to fish, she wanted to be strong and fast like the Constable and become a goddess all the same. She used to race the boys in town, promising to be faster than them someday, only to receive a broken arm from falling onto the stone path. In the days that followed, she learned about the sea, and thus began her lasting fixation.

Now, the sea provided her comfort as the town turned its back on her. Whispers that she had brought a curse on the town hovered in the air, and some claimed she had become a witch. Nothing had changed in the day-to-day of Arfiskeby. Even the priestess encouraged the town to move on, to forget Caroline's involvement, and return to their daily lives.

But the weight of the corucaish remained, even tainting her father's attentiveness, suffocating him in a wave of insouciance.

Caroline returned from her reveries to tug on her net. She braced herself for another disappointing catch.

But this time, the net held a weight.

Yet this time, the weight didn't resist her like the corucaish. Instead, it spilled out, bringing forth hundreds of fish.

Yet this time, hundreds of fish filled it.

"Oh, thank you, Constable!" she exclaimed. Then, after letting out a shriek of joy, she raced into town to tell anyone who might listen.

From that day forward, the townsfolk stopped calling her a witch; instead, she was regarded as the little fishing prodigy of the town. Caroline held the name close, wearing it like a badge of honor each day as she returned home with a net full of fish.

Soon, she knew all the best fishing spots, and a year later, when the Constable allowed her onto a boat and out to the Helvidim, she took time to learn the seas, marking each spot where the fish thrived on the map and memorizing the paths of the currents. Her crew followed, listening to her with eagerness and trust. They soon forgot the curse that she set loose with the corucaish. Even as the town grew darker and disease spiked, for a time, Caroline's name had found peace.

Yet despite the years Caroline spent mastering the boats and the sea, years away from home, she still bore her mother's name with pride. She delved into the work as a fisher, missing the festivals of Firefraught Lights each year to venture beyond the permafrost and bring back a feast for all.

And keep her family standing proud.

But she never saw another corucaish.

Nor did she ever find her mother at sea.

FIVE

As the years passed, the Firefraught Lights grew dimmer. They no longer beat with blue or gold but a dim flicker in the endless night sky. The permafrost did not glimmer with the same resolve, and tales of more silver fish reminiscent of the corucaish continued to spread between the fishing boats. Plague swept through town, killing many and leaving others faltering. Their beautiful town no longer burned like a candle but singed like a burn.

All while Caroline continued to fish.

She anxiously watched as the Firefraught Lights flickered over her boat while she returned home to Arfiskeby, glancing back at her collection of fish. A few of the other fishers stole glowers in her direction as she twiddled her thumbs. Over the past few years, she'd gathered quite the reputation as the 'conceited fishing broad.' Now past her childhood, many people asked if she would settle down and ride into the arms of marriage; her sister had even tried to pair Caroline with suitors before she moved away to the Heims Sur with her own husband. None of her efforts prevailed. Most of the suitors shied away from Caroline, wrinkling their noses at the smell of fish and seawater. Even when Victoria forced Caroline out of her fishing dress and into a handcrafted pristine one, the stench remained.

Not that Caroline minded. She held herself with disinterest, her focus maintained on one thing: finding her mother. Everyone had moved past that fateful day. Even William had moved on from his tears. He wed soon after his own eighteenth birthday, leaving Caroline the sole member of the Walsh family without a spouse.

Her father still mourned, though. Poor James Walsh never quite recovered from his wife's disappearance. He spent his days locked in prayer before disappearing at night to drink and sleep with his woes. Victoria took up the helm in the household, jading her even more, so her first gray hairs sprouted before the turn of her second decade. Caroline helped with the finances so William could go live. He studied and became a well-off tailor, able to support his pregnant wife without a fret.

With Victoria and William out of the house, Caroline knew she had to return to her father on the Night of Firefraught Lights. She couldn't leave him alone, not when the anniversary of her mother's death lingered. Caroline still refused to believe her mother had died, though. They never found the boat or other bodies. She was still out there. Lost, perhaps, but out there.

Once Caroline's boat docked, she hopped onto the pier and hurried home, past the performing fire dancers and even past her own brother sitting with his wife by the water. Seeing the town celebrate another Firefraught Night Festival brought the memories back in a wave: her mother gone, her father suffering, and her absence. *I am sorry I am late, Papa. Please be home.* She couldn't spend all night searching in brothels or pubs for her father. While she didn't dare judge her father's indulgences, a night of vices might just destroy him.

Back when Victoria and William lived with them, they would make sure he didn't wander. Caroline promised when her sister left that she would care for their father. She provided a hefty sum of money each week from the fish, but she rarely spent time at home. Her brother had moved in with his wife six months earlier, and while he came to visit, he had his own life as well. How many times had Caroline been home since then? How many times had she seen her father?

She could count them on her hands.

Her calves ached as she reached the hill where her home sat overlooking the pier. A single light twinkled from her father's window.

Relief washed over Caroline as she rushed into the house.

The relief was gone again in an instant. Except for the light creeping beneath the door to her father's room, all remained dark. It wreaked of rotting fish.

"Papa?" she called out. "I have returned!"

No response.

"Papa?" Caroline approached his bedroom door and tapped on it.

Still nothing.

Hesitantly, she pushed open the door.

Her father lay in bed, covered in warts, breaths labored, and eyes glazed in a silver plague.

SIX

Caroline raced into town. She called out, begging for help as villagers celebrated the night. Everyone avoided her, and when her attention turned to finding her brother, her search ended in failure. His little home by the water remained dark.

Sweat gathered on Caroline's brow as she rushed down the roads. Every person blended together into their colorful and ridiculous masks. She knocked into a balding man, who glowered at her with beady black eyes, but she didn't have time to apologize. *I have to find help for my father.* No one opened their hearts to her plight. The apothecary sat in darkness, while the herbalist and doctor did not show their faces when she cried.

How long had her father been sick? Had he been lying in bed for days, waiting for her? Did William know? Did anyone?

Her father had gained a reputation over the past few years. People shied away from him, spread rumors, and spoke of him in distaste. Caroline ignored how they said she was responsible. Finding the corucaish gave him the plague in their eyes. Every bad thing since that day was a part of the plague. Not just the warts, not just the sickness—everything. For years, they overlooked it because of her fishing prowess. But the truth remained in the same glares they tossed her way in childhood.

She'd found an omen.

Everything gone wrong since then led back to her.

Caroline finally found a home that still glowed with light on the opposite end of town, far away from the pier. Bile settled in her throat, and her head spun as she knocked on the door.

The curtains shuffled in the window, and a shadow peered through at Caroline. It stared at her for a moment, then the door clicked open.

A woman stood in the entranceway with red eyes. She adjusted the hair wrap on her head, eyeing Caroline up and down before grinning.

"Well, look at you. You are glowing blue," the woman said.

Caroline blinked before shaking her head. "I apologize. I do not mean to be knocking on your door at this hour. But I need help, and you are the only one not at the festival. No one seemed to care at the festival and...I am sorry...I am rambling. My father is sick, and I am clueless."

"Lucky the Constable brought you to my doorstep, Caroline. Please, come inside. I shall help." The woman beckoned.

"How do you know my name?"

"Everyone knows you."

Caroline scowled to herself, then followed the woman into the house.

The woman lived in a small shack that overlooked the evergreen forest on the south side of town. Inside, a fire flickered, warming the home to a steamy sweat. Caroline refused to remove her coat, clenching it tight around her body as she stood like a soldier by the wall.

"My name is Tilda de Locasta. Or Tilda. Or Miss Locasta. Whichever you are so inclined to use," the woman said. She had a thick accent, rich in a way that Caroline had never heard. While the people of Heims had a sharp tongue, Tilda cradled each word and carried it close to her heart.

"That is very nice, but I do not have time for formalities. I really need to help my father."

"Yes. Please sit." Tilda motioned to the table and chair by the window.

"I do not have the time!"

"Sit. I will help."

Caroline groaned, then collapsed in the chair. Tilda left the room for a moment, only to return with a small bowl. Inside, a few herbs, as well as a murky gray substance, spun.

Tilda sat down across from Caroline. "Tell me about your father."

"He is sick. That is all."

"Yes, but you need to tell me what ailment assaults him. I cannot act on the word 'sick' alone."

Caroline flushed with embarrassment. The woman didn't flinch, her red eyes continuing to scan Caroline, her full lips pulled into a frown. There was something striking about her, a type of wisdom that Caroline admired, but also a beauty behind her gaze that filled Caroline with warmth.

Tilda did not let Caroline ponder for long. "Well?"

"Oh, sards, sorry." Caroline shook her head. "He has warts all over his body."

"Go on."

"And a fever."

"Continue."

"His eyes are silver."

"Anything else?"

"He is dying! What else is there?"

"How did he acquire this illness?" Tilda pressured. "Warts, fever, dying...that could be many things."

"Why should I even trust you? You are not the apothecary!" Caroline protested. "This is useless."

"Where I come from, I studied brews and potions, knowledge and...well, cooking. Put your faith in me, Caroline Walsh. I will do my best."

Caroline sighed. "I do not know how he acquired it as I have been out at sea for the past fortnight. Yet, I can assume he got it in his late-night ventures. I am uncertain who he spends his time with or what he does, but I can only imagine. Ever since my mother's death, he has succumbed to vices and pleasures that numb his pain."

Tilda nodded and threw a few more spices into the bowl. "Very good. Very good."

Caroline waited. Tilda moved with dexterity, not even looking at the spices and herbs she added. When she stirred the mixture, she did it with a tune on her lips and a sparkle in her eyes. Time stood still.

But impatience rose as well.

How much longer would this take? As much as Caroline could watch Tilda move for hours, her father lay suffering in silence. She had to help him.

As if Tilda read Caroline's thoughts, she removed a jar and poured the thick mixture inside it. After shaking it, she handed it to Caroline. "Put this cream on your father twice a day. It should help."

"So, it will cure him?" Caroline asked.

"I can only promise it will ease his pain. Cure? As you pointed out, I am no apothecary. I can create potions, salves, and cooking, not cures." Tilda rose. "Please keep me posted on your father's progress."

"Oh."

"I apologize. But I hope it helps. Good luck."

Caroline cradled the jar close. The next morning, she would race to the apothecary, but for now, at least she had something to help her father before it was too late.

"Thank you," Caroline whispered.

"Do not dilly dally. Go." Tilda ushered Caroline to the door with a firm hand. "I wish you luck, Caroline Walsh. Stop by soon."

"I will."

Tilda smiled, then closed the door, leaving Caroline to the winter winds beneath the Firefraught Lights.

SEVEN

When Caroline returned home, she lathered her father's body in the salve. As Tilda promised, his condition improved. The next day, he sat in bed with a smile on his face but exhaustion in his eyes. He even ate a few bites of potato before sinking back to the mattress. Yet his fever didn't break, his exhaustion didn't taper, and the warts continued to grow.

Caroline ventured to the apothecary, who then came to visit her father. Yet both the apothecary and the town doctor agreed on one thing: her father had grown too ill. It was up to the Constable to decide if he would live or die.

Anger seeped through Caroline. They'd tried nothing! But she was not in a place to argue. So, for three days, she and her brother William sat by her father's side. They eased his pain with Tilda's salve, saying little, eating less, and sleeping not at all. It was just a waiting game: would the Constable save her father?

She had little faith.

Her thoughts of Tilda tore her from the pain. The woman fascinated Caroline, and while she hadn't found time to visit her again, their brief meeting haunted her. The way the woman spoke left an enchantment over her.

Almost like witchcraft.

Caroline didn't mention Tilda to her brother. She even lied and said the salve came from the apothecary just to quell her brother's worries.

Yet even the miracle of the salve dwindled, and Caroline's father deteriorated.

Three days after Caroline returned home to find her father ill, he spoke. "Caroline Elisabeth? Are you there?"

"I am here, Papa." Caroline took her father's burning hand. Her brother had gone out to get their father's affairs in order, a so-called "necessary precaution," leaving Caroline alone to tend to her father.

"Caroline," her father repeated. He did not open his eyes. "I want you to listen."

"I am listening, Papa. I am here."

He turned his head in her direction and cracked open a bloodshot eye. "Let go."

"I am sorry?"

"Let go." He closed his eyes again and said no more.

Not then.

Not ever again.

He left Caroline with those words hanging in the air, and three hours later, as the moon rose high above the permafrost, he took his last breath.

And let go.

Caroline watched him take that last breath with her brother at her side. Her heart didn't break; her tears didn't shed. At last, her father could escape the pain that had followed him all these years.

"I will write Victoria. I had already told Priestess Abernathy of our father's situation. We'll be able to send him to rest soon," William said without emotion.

Caroline nodded.

They said nothing else. Caroline rose from her spot and stepped outside, letting the brisk winter air catch her hair and lace over her skin. In the distance, fishing boats bobbed on the surface of the water, beckoning her out to sea. Had the sea not only taken her mother but her father too? If she had been home, would her father have lived?

Or did it not matter? Would fate always have a way to wring its hands around her and pull?

Shuffling caught her attention and tore her away from her thoughts. The evergreen trees creaked. A calm mist gathered at their roots.

"Hello?" Caroline called out as she approached the tree line.

Nothing.

She pushed aside the brush.

Footprints waited in the snow. Curiosity tugged her forward, and she followed them deeper and deeper into the Evergreen Forest. No one ever went this deep into the forest during the winter—not alone, at least. Why would they be out here?

She followed the footprints to the base of a towering spruce tree, where they stopped.

"Hello?" Caroline hollered again.

The only response came from the wind.

EIGHT

As they had for her mother, the town sent Caroline's father out on a pyre. Caroline stood beside William and his wife with her head bowed, not daring to make eye contact with any of the townsfolk. She overheard their remarks: "If she stayed home, her father would be alive"; "She carries the corucaish's curse"; "she should be burning out there, not her father." While she tried not to let the comments bother her, they still scratched the surface of her insecurities.

Let go.

Her father uttered those words to her. Let go of what? These remarks?

After her father's funeral, Caroline let go of her sadness and trudged into town, not staying to chat with the townsfolk who claimed they loved her father. If they loved him, they would have helped.

Instead, they let him wither, blaming Caroline for abandoning him. Hadn't she been working to support him?

Anger stabbed at her heart. *They should let go of their hatred for me. I was a child when I found the corucaish.*

Let go.

Lost in a haze of uncertainty, Caroline wandered to the part of town where Tilda's house stood, lights glimmering against the dark daytime sky. As if the woman expected Caroline, the door swung open.

"Ah, Caroline. Good day," Tilda spoke from the entrance.

Caroline grunted. "I would not call it a good day. For sard's sake, we honored my father today."

"Yes, news travels fast. I am sorry for your loss." Tilda opened the door wider. "Please come. I am sure you wish to talk."

Caroline followed Tilda into the house, uncertain if she really wanted to *talk*. So she remained quiet. With the daylight shining through the windows, Caroline absorbed the decorations. Strange plants sat on the shelf with multicolored glass orbs decorating every surface. Tilda carried a silver tea set, and without asking, offered Caroline a cup.

Caroline sniffed it, then placed it back on the table. "No, thank you."

"Ah, come. Tea has always been a delicacy where I am from."

"And where are you from?" Caroline crossed her arms. "I apologize, but I do not think I have ever seen you in town before."

"I only arrived here a few months ago after a long, harrowing journey from the south." Tilda stroked the edge of her teapot, her red eyes lost in a deep thought.

"Where, though? Kainan?"

"No, no. A country further south than that."

"Rosada?"

"No, no. Further."

Caroline shook her head. Geography had never been her strong suit, and other than the closest countries and the currents of the local sea, a thick fog masked the rest of the world.

Tilda chuckled. "I come from Gonvernnes."

"Gonvernnes?"

"Well, it is not called that anymore. It was the dominant nation on the southern continent until the Verdant War a few years ago. It has since split into Proveniro and Perennes. Have you heard of them?"

"No," Caroline said.

"No matter, no matter. Needless to say, I left. That is all." Tilda pushed the cup of tea forward. "Drink."

Caroline shoved the tea away. "I think you should tell me. Few people here are like... you."

She didn't mean it in malice. Most people in Caroline's home bore pale skin, pale eyes, and dark hair. While Tilda's dark skin certainly looked out of place, her eyes were more notable.

Her red eyes.

Her deep eyes.

Her knowing eyes.

Caroline adored them at first glance. But what would people in town think?

Tilda sighed. "Of course you continue to pry. It is not always wise, Caroline. Sometimes, it is best to keep your head to yourself. Otherwise, you never learn to let go."

Let go. Those words kept whispering to her.

"Ah, well. I shall tell you. After Gonvernnes split in its civil war, many of us left. I knew I had to come here, to Heims Norte, to your little town."

"How did you know?"

"I just did." Tilda tapped her head, then glanced at the orbs behind her, "You could say it is... magic."

"You mean... like a witch?!" Caroline fumbled backwards from her spot.

"That is one word for it, I suppose."

"Then...you are the plague on the town!"

"No, no, not like that. Not at all like that." Tilda chuckled again.

Why was she always laughing? What was so amusing?

Tilda continued, "I like to call myself a Medii or a seer. I see things beyond our world, such as ghosts and auras, knowledge, and power. I cannot cast spells. I merely...know things. Such as about you, Caroline."

"What are you implying?"

"I understand how deeply you hold your pain. You blame yourself for deaths you cannot control. In all of this, you do not dare to think about what has occurred and what will come. So instead, you push your energy into something else." Tilda reached for Caroline's hand. "I had a vision of you at sea. You must learn to let go. I can help."

Caroline pulled away, refusing to fall under this witch's spell. It'd be easy to dive into her deep red gaze, her calm voice, and her tender fingers. She couldn't, though; already, she bore a rumor on her shoulders. But to join with a witch? That would cause her demise.

Besides, Tilda knew nothing. How dare she tell Caroline any of that?

"I am leaving," Caroline stated.

"Caroline, wait!"

"Consarn it, Tilda. I said I am leaving!"

"But I want to teach you my ways."

"To be a witch?"

"To be free. Before...well, before what comes must come."

"You are speaking in riddles." Caroline turned to the door. "Goodbye, Tilda. Thank you for your help with my father. It made his last few days less painful."

She didn't wait for Tilda's response and opened the door to the brisk winter air without another word.

NINE

Caroline avoided Tilda for months, delving deeper into her desire to fish and hunt for her mother. She rarely came home, returning only once a fortnight to complete any necessary housekeeping. Despite the small size of the town, she lost contact with her brother. Rumors about her continued to grow. They called her a witch as the one who brought plague and dulled the Firefraught Lights. Yet while many people spoke of her with distaste, the town still relied on Caroline's fishing skills for food. People thrive on hypocrisy.

So Caroline thrived.

Though her heart did not.

She hardly spoke with the other fishers on her ship. Most days, she daydreamed: some days, about her mother; others, about Tilda. While she hadn't spoken to Tilda for almost a year, she observed the woman in town, gathering strange herbs and selling salves in the marketplace. Words spread that Tilda was indeed also a witch, but no one attacked her. Almost as though they feared her.

Other times, when alone in Arfiskeby, Caroline swore someone stalked her. Sometimes, she saw Tilda from afar, yet most of the time, she saw only a dark shadow vanishing into the dark day sky. Paranoia replaced Caroline's confidence, and even while out at sea, she flinched at every shadow and every voice. Who was watching her? Why?

Was it the Constable Gelida?

She sensed herself slipping beneath the pressure. At night, she paced the deck, staring at the dim outline of Firefraught Lights while nightmares of her mother, her father, and of dark shadows haunted her dreams. She wore a façade for everyone, bellowing orders and feigning confidence even as she made mistakes. The crew grew annoyed as she navigated them along the wrong strait or when they returned with half the load of fish than usual. She ignored them, trying her best to maintain composure and wear the mask of a captain, not of a struggling fisher.

I will find my mother. I will be the best. She kept reciting that promise to herself. *I will not give up.*

Yet one day, after weeks upon weeks of poor fishing and misguided attempts, Caroline arrived at the pier to prepare for another day at sea, only to find that her crew had left without her.

"No!" Caroline shouted.

A few townsfolk glanced in her direction.

"For sard's sake! How dare they, the consarn milk-sops!" she continued bellowing.

One mother covered her child's ears as they raced past Caroline. Curses continued to escape Caroline's lips until she fell to her knees, sobbing. *I need to go out to sea. I cannot stay here. I have nothing here.*

The lingering sensation of a shadow washed over her yet again. She pulled her wool cloak tight around her shoulders and glanced around. A gentle mist stroked the ground, catching locks of her hair. If only she could use the mist to disguise herself and hide her discontent— then no one in town would talk about her and the corucaish. No one would even know her name. She could move on, like a ghost, to find her mother and live her life.

Perhaps the shadows growing around her had come to take her away for that reason.

She could only pray to the Constable Gelida for that fate.

"Caroline?"

She raised her head.

Tilda knelt beside her, holding out a hand, "You do not look well, Caroline. Your aura is bleak. May I help?"

Caroline choked back her tears and took Tilda's smooth but strong hand.

"What happened, Caroline?" Tilda asked.

"The boat left without me."

"Perhaps you just need a break."

"I cannot take a break. The shadows of the corucaish's curse are closing in!"

"Shadows?"

"They watch me every day. Some days I see a figure, but most days, it is just mist and smoke." Caroline glanced over her shoulder. "Perhaps I am paranoid. But I feel it. It is growing darker by the second."

"Oh, Caroline, it is not a shadow but your fate. You should stop fighting it, my friend."

"Stop fighting what?"

"The magic."

TEN

C aroline scoffed at Tilda. Magic? Preposterous!
The Constable kept a firm watch over all
things *magic*, and anyone who dared defy her
received the clear label of "witch." Rumors followed anyone who dared to show signs of magic, chastised and
cast aside.

Yet Tilda walked with pride. Caroline had heard the
rumors, she even suspected it herself, but no one told
Tilda to leave. Without proof of magic, any evidence
came from hearsay. But now, Tilda told Caroline the
truth without flinching. She had called herself a Medii
and a seer, able to see things no one else could fathom.
Further, she claimed Caroline might be like her as well.
That was why she saw shadows and figures; that was
why her nightmares were so vivid.

Tilda showed Caroline all of this by pouring an odd silver liquid into a bowl. She added herbs and spices until an image glowed on the surface. At first, it appeared murky, but as it settled, the full picture emerged. A miniature version of Caroline filled the bowl, walking along the shoreline. Behind her, mist and shadows followed, washing over her face as temporary masks.

"Your future is filled with more than fish, Caroline. It is overflowing with prosperity." Tilda motioned to the bowl. "You shall be a brilliant woman. A powerful woman. You will become a woman who could rule the world if she dared. And I want to be by her side and help her succeed."

"That is not me. That is...a wish. A dream..." Caroline marveled at the mirage but shook her head. "That future does not belong to me."

"Says who?"

"Me. I am a fisher, a daughter, and a curse. Not...*that*."

"Is that what you are...or what you believe?"

Caroline didn't know how to reply. She bowed her head instead, twiddling her thumbs, trying to find the best answer. "I know what I am. I am the best fisher in Heims Norte. My fishing supplies the town with food—"

"That might be what you are now. But is it what you want to be?"

Caroline lowered her head. "I want to honor my family. I want to find my mother. That is who I need to be."

"The version of you who can be that is in this illusion." Tilda guided Caroline's attention back to the bowl. The miniature version of Caroline spun with mist, her bright red lips parted in a smile, blue eyes filled with excitement. Caroline touched her own pale lips. She never imagined herself with lipstick! But that lipstick, that smile...it meant more than just beauty.

"That is who I want to be."

"Then I can help you get there." Tilda held out her hand again.

This time, Caroline accepted it.

From then on, Caroline spent almost every day with Tilda. She forgot about her boat, abandoned her daily routines, and immersed herself instead in Tilda's magic. The seer taught her of magic and religions from far and wide: from the Effluvium of Rosada to the Spring Goddess of Perennes and more. She taught Caroline how to pray, how to brew, and how to envision the mist.

All of this, they completed in the shadows. If the townsfolk of Arfiskeby discovered this magic, they would send both Caroline and Tilda out to sea to drown beneath ice by the Constable's decree.

In these private lessons, Caroline's sight expanded. When she first started meeting with Tilda, a mist followed her movement, captured by shadows. But as she focused, with Tilda's help, she saw figures and people in the mist. She learned they belonged to lost souls of the dead, wandering the earth, begging for more than a disillusioned life.

When all fell quiet, Caroline stared out into the mist, searching for her father...and, despite her prayers, her mother as well.

But no one ever revealed themselves to her.

One day, sitting outside on a cold summer day, Tilda gestured to the mist. "This creates the Constable Gelida's steeds. The corucaish is born of mist. The dragons of Spinoza and Delilah far away from here live in mist. Down south, in Rosada, they pray to the mist. This mist is our life. And you, Caroline, you can control it."

"Oh, I doubt that," Caroline laughed.

"Only someone with an inclination to the mist could catch a corucaish."

"It happened when I was a child!"

"What does that have to do with anything?"

Caroline scowled to herself, then squinted into the mist. It danced before her. *I doubt I could control it, but...* She reached her hand out. The mist didn't respond.

She had learned to trust Tilda as their friendship grew. Tilda, wise beyond her twenty-seven years, understood so much more than Caroline. She'd experienced horrors from across the region, traveling through lands that feared magic, that enslaved differences, and that left children for blood. Caroline only ever feared a giant fish that ate her mother and a rumored plague spreading through town that caused the Firefraught Lights to dim. Had she seen the plague take on different forms? Yes. She saw her father die, her family grow distant, and people suffer. But this was nothing compared to Tilda.

Caroline spent days listening to Tilda's plights. She'd grown not just to admire the woman but to love and adore her. Whenever she spent time apart from Tilda, she counted the moments until she would see her friend again. When Tilda touched her skin, guided her gaze, and directed her to brew a potion, Caroline's heart fluttered. She'd never had time for love and romance, but now, Tilda drew her in by an invisible fishing rod.

"Focus," Tilda continued to reiterate each day. Caroline tried, but it grew harder. Her entire body swooned every time Tilda touched her skin.

Caroline fumbled to express her feelings, though. Every time she tried to bring up her emotions, she sank deeper into a mask of nonchalance and frustration. Tilda smiled at her, then ushered her back into her studies.

Yet even learning about magic grew dull; Caroline instead dreamt of touching Tilda's hair, of stroking her cheek and kissing her lips.

But she'd never been one for romance. Never one for emotion. She'd worn that mask her whole life.

Now, what could she say?

Tilda read Caroline like an open book, though. And one day, while Caroline stared out at sea, trying to understand the mist in the distance, Tilda took Caroline's face and planted a warm kiss on her lips.

Caroline gawked, eyes wide, mouth ajar.

"You have wanted that for a while, I know," Tilda remarked, "and I hope it shall help rid any other thoughts in your head."

"I—"

"Our romance cannot be, Caroline. At least not now."

"I—"

"Let us get back to work."

"But—"

"We do not have time, Caroline. He shall be here soon."

Caroline blinked. "I apologize...what? Who will be here soon?"

"Death."

Tilda didn't elaborate, approaching the edge of the forest where the mist hung in thick plumes.

"Wait! Tilda!" Caroline joined her. "What are you talking about?"

"I did not learn it until recently, but a vision came. The mist is drawn to you, and that is why you will one day control it. It is why the corucaish let you catch it. It is also why Death follows you." Tilda stared at Caroline with a twinge of sadness. "Death is coming for you but not to kill. It is coming to show you everything the world offers. But to succeed, you must be ready, and that is why fate brought us together. I am here to make sure you are ready to face Death."

"Death as in...the Constable Gelida?" Caroline struggled to wrap her head around what Tilda said. Her body tingled from Tilda's kiss, and every statement spun three times in her head before settling.

"No, not the Constable. Something far more powerful than her. This Death is coming to take you away, Caroline. If you learn to control the mist, you shall succeed. And I know you will succeed... so do no fret, Caroline. Do not fret at all."

ELEVEN

Death arrived in the form of a stout, balding man.

Six months after Tilda's revelation, he knocked on Caroline's front door. Those months had passed in a blur. Caroline continued to peer into the mist, trying her best to rally it around her. It would gather at her fingertips, but no matter how hard she tried, she couldn't wield it to do her bidding. Tilda cheered from the side, her gaze heavy.

At first, they didn't talk about the kiss, but a week after their lips met, they broached the subject. They could not avoid each other forever, and their desires brought them together again. Every day, Caroline swooned in Tilda's presence, and despite Tilda saying how their romance could not thrive, they found each other and shared brief moments of passion.

Yet the question remained: when would Death come knocking?

Luckily, Caroline didn't wait too long.

Caroline woke to the pounding on her door. She rubbed her eyes, then pulled on her cloak and headed to the door. The midnight summer sun glowed, causing the snow to appear yellow and the trees to dance in shades of green. She squinted as the light flooded her house.

In the doorway stood a man dressed in a black suit, his beady eyes glancing over Caroline. He stood at least half a foot shorter than Caroline, and when he stepped into the room, mist trailed behind him and caused the room to spin.

"Pardon, who are you?" Caroline blocked his path further into the house.

"Ah, good, you can see me. Tilda has done well," the man spoke in a bold accent.

"Oh, for sard's sake, it is late. Please answer the question."

The man smiled. It was the type of smile that pulled at his lips the wrong way. Rather than lighting up his eyes, the smile seemed forced and unfamiliar, as if the man hadn't smiled in years.

"Caroline Elisabeth Walsh," the man recited, "I believe you know exactly who I am."

"Humor me." Caroline reached for her fishing rod on the wall. She didn't know what good it might do, but it secured her to have some object to use as a defense.

The man sighed. "We met almost five years ago. You bumped into me and failed to apologize."

"And you come to my house in the middle of the night to tell me this? For sard's sake."

The man didn't react, continuing, "I have been observing you for five years, Caroline Elisabeth Walsh."

"Well, that is one way to make a woman quite uncomfortable."

He did not flinch at the statement. "I have watched from the shadows and from the mist."

Caroline froze. *Shadows. Watching.*

Death.

"Tilda has taught you well, Caroline. So, I am here to extend an offer," he continued.

Caroline shook her head in disbelief. *"You're* Death?"

"That is a word for it. You can call me an angel, a demon, or as we prefer to be called...a Mist Keeper."

"Mist...Keeper." Caroline recited the words, then laughed. "So you keep the mist?"

The man paced around the room, unamused. "We control the mist, and we free the souls of the dead. And I am here to offer you something beyond your wildest imagination, Caroline. You have sailed the seas, you have seen the mist, you have caught the corucaish; now I am giving you a chance to save the dead."

Caroline crossed her arms. "Elaborate."

The man placed a hand on his chest. "My name is Alojzy Goryl. I am the Seventh Member of the Council of Mist Keepers, Protectors of the Mist, Guardians of Death. I want to offer you the opportunity of a lifetime."

Caroline waited for a further explanation.

Alojzy gave her one: "I am offering you the opportunity to become my apprentice, Caroline Walsh."

"You imply I will be the apprentice to Death?"

"That...and so much more."

TWELVE

Caroline kicked Alojzy, the so-called Mist Keeper, from her house. *Apprentice to Death? Ha! What a load of malarky!* Sure, Tilda claimed Death would come knocking...but to offer her an apprenticeship? That seemed like a joke handed out by the Constable herself.

Yet the next day, Alojzy appeared everywhere. He stood in the town square, surrounded by mist. She rushed past him only to find him outside of Tilda's home. Even when Caroline entered inside and kissed Tilda on the cheek, the man watched from the mirrors, his shadow never flinching.

Caroline told Tilda everything. Tilda listened without a word, her red eyes searching every one of Caroline's movements before turning to the orbs on the wall. A sigh rippled through her body.

"I think you should listen to his offer, Caroline. This will be a chance for you to become more than your mask."

"I am not wearing a mask," Caroline groaned.

"You are. You want more. This is it, Caroline."

"But—"

"I already said that you and I had no permanent future. Death came for you, and you should follow him."

"Tilda!"

"When was the last time you took your boat out to sea, Caroline? You are no longer the star fisher. When have you last spoken with your brother or written to your sister? You have cut ties with them. We are together but only for now. I am not here to be your lover; I am here to be your guide, Caroline, and I am guiding you to Death." Tilda placed her hands on her hips and sighed. "Our futures do not exist together, Caroline. I only want the best for you."

"So going with Death is what is best for me?" Caroline snapped. "I do not even know that peculiar man!"

"You shall not just vanish. Oh, no. This is still your home for now. But Death, the man outside, will offer you the future with bright red lips. Not me. Him." Tilda took Caroline's hands. "Go. Live your best future, Caroline. That is what I have been teaching you all these years."

Caroline stared at Tilda. Was her dearest and only friend letting her go? She didn't want to leave behind everything she built.

But a life of grandeur waited for her. A life that could offer her success and answers. Might she, with Death as her master, find her mother? Could she finally bring peace to her father? Would she finally be something other than the cursed child of the corucaish and the prodigy fisher? Those were never titles she minded, but now, as she grew older, she wondered if her life could be more.

Yet did she really want to say goodbye to her home?

Tilda gripped Caroline's arm. "If you speak with him, I do not imagine you would leave today or even tomorrow. You still have much to learn, Caroline."

Caroline eyed the window. "I suppose it would not be the end of the world to hear out what this...Alojzy fellow...has to say."

"Is that his name? Alojzy?"

"That is what he said."

"Hmph. Not what I expected Death to be called."

"And what did you expect?"

"Something more...dramatic, I suppose. Then again"—Tilda's eyes twinkled as she glanced at Caroline—"the name Caroline is not quite one I would expect of Death either."

A laugh bubbled to the top of Caroline's throat. "Ah yes. If this is indeed who I am, I shall be Caroline the Nefarious Death God. Can you imagine? People will soon fear the scent of fish."

"You do smell of the sea," Tilda chuckled. "Now go. Meet this Death God named Alojzy. I will be here."

THIRTEEN

Caroline approached Alojzy on the street outside of Tilda's home.

"I am ready. I want to learn." Her voice quavered.

"Excellent. Come with me." Alojzy motioned for her to follow.

While Caroline had grown accustomed to the mist and seeing figures among it through her training with Tilda, nothing had prepared her for what Alojzy showed her.

As Alojzy walked, the mist twisted around him. It tightened, suffocating Caroline and dragging her away from the reality of Arfiskeby. Wind tugged at her hair, and a soft haze stroked her face and chin. For a moment, Caroline swore she had become more like mist than human before stabilizing in a dark tunnel before a set of towering doors. Other tunnels joined at a junction right before the doors. Except for their footsteps echoing, all remained silent.

It's like the Constable Gelida's palace. She stroked the wall beneath a glowing torch. Priestess Abernathy told the tale of the Constable Gelida's home, a palace of mazes beyond the permafrost in the land of Helvidim. Did the Constable wait for Caroline beyond those doors? Would she greet her with a smile and a prayer? Or would she turn her back on Caroline and walk away?

Alojzy's voice tore Caroline from her amazement. "Before I open the doors, I must ask. Is this the destiny you wish to pursue? For if you choose this path, there is no turning back. This will seal your fate within the year, and you will join us in your death."

Caroline furrowed her brow and eyed the doorway again. *My fate will be sealed, and I will join them in my death.* She licked her bottom lip. Hadn't she resolved herself to this when she approached Alojzy? The image of the woman in black with red-painted lips and a laugh in her throat filled her mind. That was the woman she longed to become—not the reclusive fisher, not the girl who had nightmares of her mother and father each night, not the woman who had rumors following her every movement.

She wanted to be wonderful.

"Yes." Caroline faced Alojzy. "I accept whatever fate may come."

"You understand that may mean your death?"

"I do."

"Excellent." Alojzy turned to the door, and as if on command, it opened. Mist surged into the junction.

On the other side, the glow of a silver chandelier greeted her. Its lighting engulfed the entranceway, drawing Caroline's attention to the immense bookshelves forming queues throughout the room. Upon them sat more books than Caroline ever imagined.

Although, she would be the first to admit she'd only visited a library once before in her life.

It didn't stop her from marveling as she walked into this mysterious library, though. She ran her fingers along the shelves before glancing up towards the incandescent glass walkways above the heart of the library. Multicolored mist danced through the air, and a few dead souls wandered about, carrying books and humming to the tune of the wind.

Alojzy moved to Caroline's side. "I built this, the Library of the Council, over the last couple hundred years."

"You built this?" Caroline reiterated.

"Yes. It is my talent."

"Your talent?"

"My talent with the mist."

"Talent with the mist. You imply... magic?"

"Yes, magic. It is a fickle yet powerful thing. It is far more intricate and worthy than the simple magic used by seers and witches. We can do anything if we put our minds to it."

"We." Caroline let that word hang on her tongue.

Alojzy took that statement as a question. "The Council of Mist Keepers, whom you will serve as a member if you succeed."

Caroline shook her head, stroking her fingers along the spines of the books. "The Council of Mist Keepers?"

"There are seven of us currently as full members. You shall join us as the eighth member. In due time, you will meet us all, learn from us all, and grow. Together, we protect this world of mist, save the souls of the dead, and guard our magic and talents against those who might use it wrong. We are the masters of this world." Alojzy removed a book from the shelf and blew off the dust. "And we have more knowledge than you could ever imagine."

Caroline stared at the book in his hand, then up at the incandescent ceiling above her. Made of glass, it sparkled with the beat of every second, almost singing a quiet tune of mist and magic, beckoning for Caroline to join it.

Yet, as she marveled at the mist gathering around the platform and around Alojzy, her heart sank. She'd tried to control it, tried to understand it, but the mist never obeyed.

"What if I cannot learn to harness this power?" Caroline asked Alojzy.

The man's face grew dark, eyes steady. "You will harness it."

"And if I cannot?"

"Then I have failed you as a teacher. But I promise that I have always succeeded."

FOURTEEN

Alojzy trained Caroline with the intensity and determination of a corucaish. Every day, Caroline followed Alojzy as he traveled through the mist-filled tunnels beneath the earth, arriving in different locations across the globe where the dead rested. With a firm hand, Alojzy taught Caroline how to release the souls of the dead, telling her to search for their cries as they begged from the mist to help.

Caroline never heard the cries. She followed with uncertainty. How did Alojzy hear the sobs?

She only felt the wind brushing her face.

All while inhaling the putrid scent of death.

Once again, she reminded herself of what her mother told her long ago when she shied from the scent of fish.

Focus on your favorite smell. Keep it right in your mind. Let it overwhelm you. That is your essence.

That is the essence of death.

Over time, the stench dulled, and she could instead focus on Alojzy's lesson, taking every word in stride. When she wasn't with him or visiting with Tilda to recount her day, she waited in the Library as different Mist Keepers introduced themselves to her. She first met Aelia, who used the mist to heal, followed by Tomás, who had the innate ability to read and interpret the mind. They spoke cordially, offering their assistance where needed, before venturing into the shelves.

Caroline briefly met Malaika, who created maps with the mist, only to vanish for weeks after their meeting. The giant, Jiang, would scoff at Malaika and said to Caroline, "If you end up like her at all, I might just throw you off the balcony. Behave yourself, girl."

Caroline almost told the giant off, but a white-haired Mist Keeper with beautiful green eyes named Julietta tugged the giant away by his arm. The woman walked with a sway in her hips, her long white hair falling down her back like waves.

She reminds me of the Constable Gelida. While the Constable bore many descriptions, Julietta's beauty captured everything Caroline kept close about the Constable: enigmatic, poised, and beautiful. She struggled to find her voice when she met Julietta for the first time, gaping as the woman strode away.

Yet of all the Mist Keepers, the one that shocked Caroline the most had to be the leader himself, Ningursu. When Caroline first met him, she almost started laughing. Ningursu was none other than a head, part skull and part skin, resting upon a pillow. When he spoke, his voice boomed.

The entire Council of Mist Keepers obeyed him without question.

Caroline admired his tenacity and leadership. She, too, would follow.

Well, if she survived her training.

"Recite their names and talents again," Alojzy ordered as they wandered through the tunnels.

Caroline huffed, then said, "Ningursu was the first Mist Keeper, and he uses the mist to maintain control. Next came Aelia, who can use the mist to heal. Then there's Tomás, who uses the mist to delve into minds. Next comes"—her stomach flipped—"Julietta, who can paint the world with mist. She then trained the giant Jiang," she snarled his name, "who only dares release souls and nothing else. He trained Malaika, who uses the mist as a map. Then there's you, Alojzy, the architect of the mist."

"Very good."

"But what does that matter if I cannot harness the mist?" Caroline spat. "We have been training for months. Yes, I can release souls; that has been easy. You just reach for them and pull them free. But finding the souls... How can I be a Mist Keeper if I cannot *find* the dead?"

"You will find them. If Malaika could find them, you can.".

Caroline grumbled. Malaika had a reputation for getting lost, but she at least proved to be a successful Mist Keeper. Even after months—or years, if she counted her training with Tilda—she could not harness the mist. What would she do if her time came to join the Mist Keepers and she wasn't ready?

Alojzy never elaborated on when her time would come. She'd already realized becoming a Mist Keeper meant abandoning everything in her life. But when would that be?

Alojzy remained elusive, continuing to coach her in the art of releasing souls. It was a simple job, really. Caroline approached the dead, where their soul waited deep in the confines of their mind—or personal Hell—and reached through the mist for their soul. She yanked it out of the dark abyss, searching the mist for their faces. The soul then solidified before her, joining at last with the mist. Free to be...free to live.

But she still couldn't find the souls. That fell on Alojzy.

"You keep telling me to harness the mist, but I do not understand what that means," Caroline said to Alojzy as they walked. "Please... give me a hint."

He said not a word.

"Alojzy! Please! I do not want to fail you."

He trailed a few paces ahead into the mist, letting the darkness wash over him.

"Alojzy!" Caroline chased after him.

As she walked forward, the mist thickened into a deep miasma of uncertainty. She could no longer see Alojzy or the walls of the tunnels. Truth be told, she couldn't see anything. Where was she supposed to go now?

"Oh, for sard's sake..." She felt for a wall, or any surface, really, but the mist provided no escape. She cursed beneath her breath as she fumbled along in search of her master. Was this his way of saying that her final trial had arrived? Or had he given up on her and her inability to find the deceased?

She held out her hands as she walked. *Focus on the mist. Listen for the cries of the dead.* Caroline strained her ears. No sound. No screams. Nothing but the wind stroking her face, tugging at her chin, and guiding her.

Guiding.

Guiding...

Caroline blinked. A man's face appeared. She'd never seen the man before, with his wide nose and bushy mustache. The mist cradled the image before her for a moment, then sent it flying into the darkness.

"Wait!" she cried and raced after it.

The image remained in the forefront of her mind, and her intuition led her out of the tunnels and into the daylight. A graveyard with silver bells attached to the headstones greeted her. They opened their arms to her, beckoning her forward, and she obliged.

A newer headstone sat towards the back of the graveyard. Here, the image of the man with the crooked nose solidified.

He is here. Set him free.

She did as Alojzy had taught her moons ago and placed her hand in the dirt. The man's soul tingled to the surface, then shot outwards and into the mist.

The image in Caroline's mind's eye dissipated.

"Very good, Caroline," Alojzy spoke from behind her.

Caroline turned, a scream rising in her throat. "How dare you—"

She stopped. Alojzy stared at her with his eyebrows raised, a grimace crossing his lips.

"What?" she snapped.

"Your face."

"What about it?"

"Here. Come look at yourself." Alojzy guided her to one of the silver bells by the graves.

Caroline glanced at her reflection.

Except she didn't stare back.

Instead, the face of the man she had released stared at her like a mask woven onto her skin with mist. Caroline shook her head a couple times, and when the mist finally let go of her cheeks, her own face returned. She poked her skin.

"It appears you can create illusions and masks to hide yourself as well as identify those who require your services," Alojzy stated. "The mist is yours now, Caroline. You are ready."

FIFTEEN

Caroline continued to practice for weeks. Despite being 'ready,' it was not her time yet to take over for Alojzy. He told her that she would know when it was time. Truthfully, Caroline wasn't in a rush to become a Mist Keeper. She instead focused on fine-tuning her masks until she was able to disguise herself as an old woman, a young man, and even wear the image of a hound on her face. Each day, she tried to be a different person...at least until Death beckoned her to release a soul into the Constable's misty embrace.

She loved showing Tilda her newfound ability, making her dearest friend laugh with the new faces while they gossiped about the occurrences both in and out of town. Things had grown bleak over the years; the winter nights lasted longer, and the Firefraught Lights did little to lighten the paths. The plagues that went through town remained.

Caroline soon took up the reins at night to release the souls of the dead in Arfiskeby. With the mist as her cloak, she moved like a shadow, all while keeping a single desire in the back of her mind: finding her father and mother. She never found them, though.

Instead, she alone controlled the mist in Arfiskeby.

Alone.

Always alone.

Her solitude echoed around her as she released souls at night. Soon, she would be without Tilda. No one else would mourn her when she passed. After all, she hadn't spoken to her brother William in years, nor had she written to her sister Victoria. They had families now, new lives.

So did Caroline.

One day, while sitting in the parlor drinking tea, Tilda remarked, "I fear our time is ending, Caroline. You will go on to the Mist Keepers...and I have elsewhere to travel."

Caroline's heart sank, but she didn't argue with Tilda. She felt it, too. The mist grew thicker by the day. She could sense souls calling to her from across continents.

Soon, she would take the torch from Alojzy.

Although Caroline bubbled with excitement over the possibilities, melancholy filled her heart as well. She'd abandoned her love of fishing and immersed herself in the world of the mist. While she kept thoughts of her mother close, she had no more answers than she did as a child. What if she'd never met Tilda or Alojzy? Would she have found her mother yet?

Tilda pulled Caroline from her reveries. "Come with me to the market, Caroline. I must get some new herbs."

"I wish I could, dear Tilda, but Alojzy—"

"You will have centuries with that man, Caroline. Please humor me. I want to see what they have." Tilda motioned Caroline towards the door as she pulled on her cloak. "Please?"

Caroline frowned, then nodded slightly. How much time did she have left with Tilda, after all?

They walked side-by-side down the road towards the pier. Outside, they rarely held hands or showed affection. It wasn't proper; the Constable looked down upon any public displays of affection. Yet Tilda kept her shoulder close to Caroline, peering at the dark day sky, snow flurries hitting her tightly bound hair.

"I often wonder what I am going to do after all of this," Tilda whispered.

"You can continue to make salves, continue to live," Caroline replied. "You are quite talented, after all."

"Making salves? There is so much more to this world, Caroline. I do not see that as my future." Tilda stared ahead at the pier where droves of individuals gathered. "For many years now, I have had sight as a guide thanks to my silver pools. I knew to come here, I knew to find you, but now mist shrouds the future. Soon, it will be time for me to unlock my future. My talents know no limits. I think I may be able to do more with what I see. Perhaps I could help people find their truth...or solve mysteries!"

"You wish to be a detective?" Caroline chuckled.

"Perhaps." Tilda gripped Caroline's arm and laughed. "Perhaps I do."

They walked in silence, arm in arm, for a few moments. More commotion filled the pier where the boats docked. The mist tugged at Caroline as she approached, and a knot formed in her stomach.

At the edge of the docks, upon a fishing hook, hung none other than a corucaish. From its mouth swung the head of a fisher who once served on the same boat as Caroline.

The mist pulled Caroline towards the scene. She didn't hear Tilda call out to her, nor did she hear the gasps that echoed across the pier. One step at a time, she approached the man's head, eyes wide and mouth ajar. His soul reached for her.

And she reached back for it.

Until a young girl screamed.

"She took his face!"

Caroline stopped. With a trembling hand, she touched her face. Stubble rested on it, as well as a wide nose and chapped lips. The soul of the dead still beckoned her, but she could not act.

Instead, Caroline stepped away from the corucaish. She waved her hand, and mist gathered at her fingertips. Her mask slipped away.

And she stood alone.

Vulnerable.

Caroline turned to glance back at Tilda. Her dearest friend had vanished into the growing crowd.

So she stood alone against everyone with the little girls crying out the word everyone believed:

"Witch."

SIXTEEN

The town locked Caroline in a cell made of lead where old Priestess Abernathy came with a final prayer. The words hung with Caroline's sealed fate.

No one defended her.

No one came to visit.

Tilda had left.

Alojzy had nothing to say.

And her family...well, she lost them years ago.

Caroline, alone, waited in the cell for her death sentence: witches, per the Constable's decree, must drown. There was no exception.

Everyone saw her magic. Even now, every so often, her face shifted with the mask of the dead. She had no way to escape. The mist did not welcome her into the tunnels or through the doors. She was trapped, locked away from the world, rotting.

Until the door opened.

She didn't fight as Priestess Abernathy led her out to the pier.

Nor did Caroline fight as the strongest men in town tied her to blocks of lead.

The town had seen her under the guise of witchcraft.

If she had to succumb to this trial, so be it.

Her old fishing crew carried her out past the permafrost. The brisk winter air stroked her ever-changing face, and the song of the Constable Gelida haunted the landscape with a quiet hum. Caroline didn't speak with her old crew, watching as they pushed past the permafrost beneath the glowering Firefraught Lights.

I should have known I would succumb to the Constable's wrath eventually. The corucaish has marked me, and this is my destiny. I cannot fight this.

I am so sorry, Mama.

Thoughts of her mother broke Caroline's heart. She never found her like she'd promised William and herself. She had an eternity still, she supposed, but even an eternity might not be enough time.

The boat skidded at the edge of the permafrost, looking out into the dark waters at the end of the world. Caroline nodded toward the midnight horizon. The mist opened its arms. She could see it, waiting, like the Constable throwing her arms open for an embrace.

Caroline's old crew threw down their anchors, then hoisted Caroline up from her spot. She walked forward with the lead anchors and weights trailing behind her.

No fussing.

No fighting.

This was her fate.

They led her to the edge of the boat.

No one spoke.

Caroline lowered her head. She didn't have any last words. After all, if she believed in everything Alojzy taught her, this was just the beginning.

She had to put her faith in the mist.

And perhaps the Constable as well.

Balancing on the side of the boat, she glanced back at her old crew. It was a shame, really; she only knew them by face and not by name. It had been like that since she boarded her first boat. She was the prodigy, the guide, and the curse; it was best to let her do her job, and the crew would do their work.

Then they abandoned her.

No camaraderie.

No friendship.

Now, they pushed her from the boat without a second thought.

It happened at once, no celebratory remarks or last wishes.

Caroline fell to the water, and the permafrost cracked. She did not have the strength to fight the lead as it pulled her deep beneath the water's surface.

Freezing.

Clawing.

She gasped, and water filled her lungs.

Her vision darkened.

And her life ended on the floor of the sea.

SEVENTEEN

D eath came with darkness.
               Loneliness.
           And obsolescence.

Caroline was nothing.

And that froze the last pieces of her heart.

She wandered in the darkness, searching... begging... demanding light.

An identity.

A chance to apologize.

But she only met water and fear.

Drowning...
      Drowning...
           Drowning...

It happened again.

And again.

Nothingness.

Emptiness.

Forgetfulness.

As she wandered, she found a mirror in the darkness.

A single light glimmered.

Whose face did she wear? She did not recognize the eyes staring back.

Black? Brown? Green? Blue?

Each time, she met a different hue.

How could she escape?

Darkness.

Emptiness.

She begged.

She pleaded.

The circle continued.

Escape.

She needed to escape.

No voices spoke to her.

No maps guided her path.

No stories guided her to salvation.

But Caroline saw faces.

They smiled and held open arms.

They waited for her.

They yearned to help her.

Where?

Where to go?

How?

Walk. Hope.

Succeed.

She pictured the face of the woman with the red lips.

And that woman would climb out of Hell.

She would kick.

She would scream.

So Caroline did.

Until, at last, the woman with red lips appeared and offered her a hand.

She took it.

The woman tugged her towards a distant light.

And Caroline was free.

EIGHTEEN

Caroline gasped, sputtering as water filled her mouth.

Yet, she wasn't drowning.

Rather, she was floating.

She swam out of her personal Hell, deep within the confines of her mind, following the woman with red lips. The mist welcomed her into its embrace. Through the murky water, she swam, inhaling and exhaling the water and thriving on her own death.

Until the water broke, and she came up for air in a tunnel.

She splashed to the surface in a dark cave. Grabbing hold of a nearby stalagmite, she yanked herself ashore. With a gasp, she rolled over onto her back, raising her hands in front of her face in the dim, flickering light.

Black and blue splotches covered her skin.

I did it. I escaped my mind. I am a Mist Keeper.

Alojzy had recited repeatedly how she would have to escape Hell on her own if she wanted to become a Mist Keeper. She hadn't expected such a horrendous scene. She should have, she knew, especially after all the releases she'd completed. But it wasn't like she experienced their Hell; she saw only a brief glimpse of their faces, writhing in pain.

To feel each version of Hell would be torture. Hers alone left her quivering.

Forgotten.

Nothing.

After regaining her footing, she limped deeper into the cave until it transformed into one of the Mist Keeper tunnels. She followed her instinct, letting it guide her inwards towards the junction. With every few steps, she coughed up water. Her clothes dripped, and her hair stuck to her head. She couldn't tell how long she'd been underwater. Hell felt like ages. But it might have been moments, minutes, days, weeks... or months. Perhaps longer.

Did the Council of Mist Keepers wait for her?

Did they even know she had died?

As she reached the junction, the door to the Library swung open as if honoring her arrival. She straightened her back and approached, holding her breath. Was the Council waiting for her, ready to welcome her to eternity? She could only imagine their smiles: the next Mist Keeper, joining them at last.

Well, she couldn't really imagine any of them smiling. Did any of them ever show emotion? They all were ever so droll and staid. No laughter, no smiles, no...nothing.

So, it didn't surprise Caroline that no one waited for her but the glistening floors of the Library.

She dawdled along the pathway towards the galley in the back of the Library. If anything, she would snag some food and find a place to wait. Someone had to show up, eventually.

Yet the galley also sat silent. *Do I even need to eat if I am dead?* Caroline wondered. Yet becoming a Mist Keeper, she also knew, wasn't a true death. It was just another plane of existence, one where the Constable Gelida might walk and thrive. Food, she supposed, was still necessary.

Caroline snagged a silver plate from the countertop and headed to the pantry.

Her own reflection caused her to stop.

She gasped.

Staring back at her was not *her* face. Rather, a sea monster gaped back at her, with blotched skin hanging from her bones. Only her blue eyes held any semblance of her past self. No red lips. No prominent nose. No thin eyebrows.

She had melted away, worn down by the salt and the sea.

Caroline dropped the plate with a crash. The pieces shattered around her feet, and she toppled back against the counter, staring wide at her hands. Her mind spun. *How long was I underwater? Why did I not come back as a Mist Keeper?*

"Oy! What's going on in there?" A deep voice bellowed.

Jiang the Giant marched into the galley. When he caught sight of Caroline, a smirk traveled over his lips. "Ah, I see you finally figured your way out. Alojzy believed you would do it... but I thought you'd flub it."

Caroline glowered at him.

Jiang continued, "Though you do kind of look like an ogre now. Guess you didn't turn out as perfect as Alojzy hoped."

"What is that supposed to mean?" Caroline snapped.

"If you were perfect, you would have gotten out within hours. Not weeks. But Alojzy held out for you, and I guess it's good... seeing as you did it. Oh, joy. He's going to rub that in everyone's faces; he's the first master to succeed on his first apprentice. It takes a few tries for most of us to get it right." Jiang leaned against the counter. "At least you didn't meet *all* his expectations. And now, looking like this...ha! To think the petty living already tells horrors about Death. Now they'll speak of the evil ogre!"

"Be quiet," Caroline snarled.

"What are you going to do? Change my face?" Jiang leaned forward on his heels. "Your magic isn't all that strong, Caroline."

"At least it is stronger than yours."

"What are you saying?"

"Alojzy told me about your magic," Caroline stepped forward. "He said that you are too afraid to use the mist. You can just release souls, and that is it."

Jiang clenched his fists tight. "I can still snap you in half."

"I doubt the others would be a fan of that."

"Oh? Try me."

Just as Caroline stepped forward, another individual entered the doorway. Caroline's stomach fell.

Julietta entered the room as if on a cloud. Her purple dress, stained with paint, gathered at her feet, and a soft smile tugged at her lips. It was a true smile, one that Caroline had hoped to see upon arriving.

Not forced.

Not pernicious.

True.

"Caroline," Julietta sang, "I am so happy you have returned to the Library."

"I only returned a couple hours ago," Caroline replied, stealing one last glare at Jiang.

"Well, I hope you two have not gotten into too much trouble."

"Hmph," Jiang grumbled.

Julietta continued, unphased, "Has Al been around to help you prepare?"

"No. I have not seen him." Caroline said.

"Ah, very well. I can help then."

"Julietta, is that wise?" Jiang asked, a softer tone creeping into his words.

"I know what is best for me, Jiang. After all, I am your master." Julietta waved Caroline out of the galley. "Come. I'll show you to your room."

Caroline stuck her tongue out at Jiang, then followed Julietta from the room. Yet even as she left behind her reflection, her body continued to shake with anger and fear. Was this the fate the Constable Gelida cursed her with, after all these years, to live an eternity with the face of a sea monster?

Why?

What had she done wrong but catch a corucaish as a child?

Nineteen

Julietta led Caroline to the suite Alojzy had prepared on the first floor of the Library. It connected to a tunnel that led to the Rosadian Sea, overlooking a miasma of color and awe. Fishing nets and rods hung on the wall, intermingling with the bookshelves and desk. Two large sofas filled the room, while a door on the far wall led her own private quarters to a canopy bed.

As soon as Caroline sat on the bed, she collapsed, unaware of how much of a toll the escape from Hell had on her body. She slept for days surrounded by nightmares, only to be awoken when Julietta brought her food or when Aelia, the Healer, returned with an elixir for her consistent headache.

After a week went by, Caroline finally climbed out of bed. Julietta waited in Caroline's office, painting a mural of the sea on the wall.

"Oh, you have awoken, I see." Julietta smiled in Caroline's direction. Paints smudged her skin. As she spoke, the mural on the wall moved.

Caroline blinked, then asked, "What are you doing here?"

"Oh, I thought your room needed to be prettier. It was so bland. Al never considers *personal* touches. All work, no play." Julietta placed her paintbrush in a large pocket in her dress. She continued, "But we have to work, as it seems. That is really why I'm here."

"Where is Alojzy, though? Should he not be helping?"

"He has completed what he must with you, and I volunteered to instruct you in the rest. Now what was I going to say? One moment..." She wrung her hands together, glanced at the painting, then nodded. "Ah yes. Your paths."

"My paths?"

"As in... your routine. What you need to get done each day."

"You mean releasing souls?"

"Yes. That is what I mean, yes." Julietta's brow furrowed, and she brushed back a strand of hair from her pink cheeks. "You know about that?"

Caroline nodded. Alojzy had told her how she would need to release a certain number of souls each day to keep the world at peace. She could develop her own routes and find the best option available for her. None of what Julietta said was new.

"Right. Of course you do," Julietta said. "Well...Malaika sewed a cloak for you, and there is some other clothing in your room. I expect you to know what you like to wear; I would hate to put you in something you'd hate."

"Yes, thank you."

"Once you're ready, I'll be here. Al asked me to help you these first few days. Said it would be good..." Julietta kept fidgeting, moving her fingers from her hair to her nose, then to tug at the loose thread on her sleeve.

Caroline thanked Julietta one last time before returning to her sleeping quarters. In the closet, a beautiful cloak hung, knitted with a pattern of waves and sea. In a certain light, the threads glimmered blue, but otherwise, it hung like the dark night sky with no Firefraught Lights. She removed it, as well as a simple white and red dress.

She glimpsed herself in the mirror as she got ready. Her face continued to hang, blotched and bruised, with her blue eyes shining. Her hair had turned gray from lack of sunlight, hanging like seaweed on her head. Caroline pulled at a strand, willing it to curl again, but it only fell back against her shoulder in a pathetic sigh.

Frustration mounted within her stomach and, in a fit of spontaneity, she threw her shoe at the mirror. The object cracked, further damaging her own reflection.

She turned her back on it and dressed in a hurry. The material warmed her skin, and for a moment, Caroline imagined herself back home, walking along with Tilda, laughing and smiling.

Then it faded, and she stood alone in the office.

She hurried to pull up the hood of her cloak. It did well enough to hide her face.

Perhaps if she imagined hard enough, she would become the woman with red lips from Tilda's basin.

Or at least she could pretend.

TWENTY

For months, Julietta helped Caroline with completing her soul releases. It started as a cordial arrangement on the first day; Julietta helped Caroline create a routine. Each word she spoke calmed Caroline. And as they traveled, as they worked, Caroline grew more attached to the woman. They became inseparable, and despite how Caroline's face continued to slip into an unrecognizable mask, Julietta didn't flinch. Each day came with smiles. They shared laughter as Julietta slipped into the sea when Caroline taught her how to fish, as well as when Caroline attempted to paint a portrait of Julietta.

For the most part, Caroline never saw Alojzy, nor did she see most other Mist Keepers. Many kept to themselves, except for Jiang the Giant, who often mocked

Caroline as she walked past, swinging the canteen on his hip with a dramatic twirl. Caroline glowered at him, but to keep Julietta happy, she tried not to engage with him.

Tomás, the empathetic Mist Keeper with the ability to read minds and emotions, often visited as well. He would sit cross-legged in Caroline's office and talk, analyzing her emotions and infiltrating her mind. She hated the way he pried, but she never pushed him away, either. Something soothing followed Tomás as he walked, and part of Caroline grew more confident after every conversation.

Hold on to your constant, he always said. *It will help you thrive.*

Except Caroline struggled to find her constant. What had always stayed by her side? She lost her mother, her father, her siblings, and Tilda. She still fished, but how did that soothe her? In some ways, fishing caused more trouble than it was worth ever since she found the corucaish.

She had nothing.

Except Julietta.

But was she a constant in Caroline's life?

She pondered this question daily; whether she walked from soul to soul, or changed her clothes, or sat with Julietta beneath a banyan tree, she constantly wondered.

Caroline stood before her mirror, poking at her skin with the question lingering. Julietta entered without knocking. A usual occurrence, Caroline didn't even flinch, obsessed instead with the way the skin flopped from her chin.

"I've told you, Caroline, you are still perfect in every way," Julietta remarked.

Caroline shook her head.

"You do, though."

"You say that, but I go through every day looking like a sea monster! I do not feel human!" Caroline cursed, "For sard's sake, Julietta. It might be vain, it might be self-deprecating, but I want to feel *human* again."

"You are human."

"I am a monster."

"Well, you are Death," Julietta giggled, then caught herself, "but I understand. You do not want people to fear you after you have saved them from eternal damnation, yes?"

Caroline wiped her eyes. More often than she could count, so many souls quivered in horror. Why should they trust the creature, welcoming them into the other world? Julietta had a guise of kindness, Alojzy had an assertive hand, and even Jiang had a smile that wooed the heart at first glance.

What did Caroline have but a melted face?

Julietta placed a hand on Caroline's shoulder. "Listen to me. I came today to tell you that Alojzy told me that Ningursu told him...it is time for you to complete your releases unassisted."

Caroline spun to meet Julietta. "What!?! No... I cannot be ready! I have only been doing this for a couple of months! What if they flee from me? Julietta, you are the kindness to my monstrosity! Please... I do not want to do this alone."

"But you already have been, Caroline. All I do is walk beside you... I believe, yes. That is what I have done. As I did before..." Julietta's face grew distant, and she mumbled something in Spinozan under her breath.

Caroline gulped back the tears filling her throat. She refused to cry; she hadn't cried at her own mother's funeral, and she wouldn't cry now. Julietta would be in the Library waiting for her when she got back from her routes. It wasn't like they were abandoning her.

She'd never be alone again. The Council of Mist Keepers would stay by her side through everything.

But her throat continued to tighten.

"I cannot do this alone," Caroline bemoaned. "I thought when I became a Mist Keeper, I would be this powerful woman with gorgeous red lips, pristine hair, and ferocity behind her. I thought I would finally find my place... but I am empty. I am not the woman Tilda showed me, Julietta! I am just... a creature from the sea. Like a corucaish."

"But unlike the corucaish, you can paint your own future."

"Oh, for sard's sake, that is preposterous!"

"But it is the truth."

"Oh, shut it!" As Caroline shouted, mist rose at her feet. She kicked it away. She didn't have the heart to release souls. They could wait.

Julietta stared at Caroline, a half-smile drizzling over her lips. She removed the paintbrush from behind her dress pocket and waved it through the air before saying, "Oh Caroline, you are ever so dramatic."

"I am not being dramatic!"

"You are a bit of a drama queen, dear."

"I thought you were on my side!"

"I am. But Caroline, if only you took a moment to think. Come." Julietta led Caroline back towards the mirror.

Caroline didn't dare peer at her own reflection, glowering instead at the ground as she followed her friend.

"Please, look." Julietta urged.

"I know what my face looks like. I do not need your sympathy."

"But Caroline... you need to look." Julietta tugged at Caroline's hand.

"Fine!" Caroline snapped, then pulled her attention away from the ground to her reflection.

This time, her heart stopped.

Not out of fear or sadness, but in utter awe.

Pulsing with mist, her face had transformed. Her hair once again hung in thick black strands, her skin glimmered with a smooth tone, and her lips had filled out, ready for the red paint from Tilda's vision. Caroline placed her hand on the mirror, then reached up to touch her own cheeks. Mist gathered at her fingertips, but it didn't shift.

This mask permanently sat on her face.

"You painted your face back on!" Julietta exclaimed.

Caroline poked again at her face. It still didn't budge.

She glanced back at Julietta. "I have my face again."

"I told you that you were no monster. Now... you are your destiny."

TWENTY-ONE

Caroline's new face injected her with newfound confidence. She greeted each day by readjusting her mask, willing the mist into place before completing her routes. It took a few days to get used to applying her face, but once it became a part of her rhythm, it was as easy as brushing her hair. When she first developed the face, she had to check after every few soul releases that it returned, but to her surprise and relief, it was no temporary marking. Rather, it existed as an extension of herself.

Serving as a Mist Keeper suddenly became, well, a dream. She was the woman in black, walking through the world with the years passing, releasing souls without circumstance. Mostly, the Council existed as a quiet utopia. Ningursu stayed out of Caroline's affairs, as long as she did her job, while Alojzy rarely checked on her. The others popped in and out, with Tomás checking in once a month on Caroline's "psychological health," as he called it. Caroline ignored it, focusing instead on completing her job.

And being the best.

Only Jiang and Julietta stayed as constant elements in her life. Jiang loved to toy with her, mocking her movements or throwing a snide remark in her direction about some minor mistake. He said it was all in good fun, but every time he spoke, it left her on ice.

"Malaika spent all that time making that cloak for you, and you up and got it covered in mud," Jiang snarled one day while passing Caroline on the steps.

Caroline glowered in his direction. "Well, at least she made me a cloak. What do you have?"

"I have what I need," Jiang replied, adjusting the sleeves of his shirt.

"It does not appear you have any friends, though. Your own apprentice, Malaika, avoids you! I would have thought you two would be thick as thieves."

"You do not seem close to Alojzy."

"That means nothing. He and I have a formal relationship."

"Who is to say it is not the same with Malaika?"

"It is quite obvious that she does not particularly enjoy your company." Caroline stepped towards him. "No one does, Jiang. You are always making shrewd remarks. Do you have any friends?"

Jiang stared hard at Caroline. His green eyes grew dark, his lips fell into a straight line, and with a single puff of air, he sucked in his lips. Then he stepped forward. His footsteps rocked the pathway, causing the multicolored glass beneath his feet to transform from a soft blue to a vivid red.

"Do *you* have friends?" He asked, his voice booming like thunder.

"Well... Julietta." Caroline scoffed.

"Is she really *your* friend?"

"But of course!"

"What do you know about her? Is she not someone you just rant to and weigh down with your own self-pity? Come now. Tell me one detailed thing about Julietta."

Caroline's stomach formed a knot. She could feel her face flicker as the uncertainty nestled over her. *One thing.* She licked her lips. It had been almost a decade; certainly, she knew things about Julietta! The woman had done so much for her.

One thing.

Caroline gulped, then in a voice as quiet as a mouse, she said, "She hails from Spinoza."

"Go on." Jiang crossed his arms.

"And... her favorite color is purple." Caroline kept her voice level. "She is a talented painter and would rather make a mess while painting than keep her workspace pristine."

"Anything else?"

"Well, um, she is quite kind and thoughtful and—"

"You know nothing of her," Jiang barked. "Nothing! She knows every little part about you, but you do not know a thing! So let me tell you—"

"You do not know anything either, Jiang!" Caroline interjected.

"Oh, but I was her apprentice. I know so much about the failures she holds close to her chest. I know how much she forgets in hopes of making her heart content. But you do not know about that, do you? Because you are too busy mulling about your own problems!" Jiang leaned back on his heels. "She is not your savior. You are using her."

"I am not!" Caroline spat.

"You are."

"No—"

"Jiang? What is going on?" Julietta's sing-song voice cut through the arguments.

She waltzed down from the third floor of the Library, her purple dress like a cloud behind her. Caroline's heart still skipped upon seeing Julietta, her long hair falling like waves on her shoulders, her green eyes wide like the sea. They spent so much time together, more time than Caroline spent with anyone in her life, but Caroline couldn't gather the courage to say how much Julietta warmed her heart. The woman was centuries older than her, had lived so many more lifetimes, and encountered so many possibilities. Why would she even look at Caroline as more than a child?

After all, the Council treated her as a mere child with no knowledge, waiting for answers to be handed on a silver platter.

Jiang finally responded to Julietta, "Nothing. Caroline and I were only having a civil conversation."

Caroline glowered at Jiang but didn't reply.

"Oh, well, good." Julietta joined them at the bottom of the stairs. "I appreciate that you two are getting along."

"Yes, we are." Jiang kept his voice level. "But I must go for now. I shall visit with you later, Julietta."

"Very well. Tea later?"

"Do you not remember? I do not drink tea. Perhaps a glass of red wine."

"I will have a bottle prepared."

"No, that is okay. I shall bring my own." With that statement, Jiang walked away, leaving Caroline and Julietta alone on the stairs.

Julietta blinked a couple times, then nodded. "That's right. He likes his special brew..."

Her face fell hollow, bottom lip quivering. Caroline watched her, unsure what to say, Jiang's words still hanging heavily over her heart. *I know the failures she holds close to her chest. I know how much she forgets.* What did he mean by that? Julietta always carried an air of serenity; what would haunt her?

Julietta's face broke into a sudden smile, and she glanced at Caroline, a childish expression glistening in her green eyes. "Are you finished with your routes for today, Caroline? Shall we go walk?"

"Oh, um, yes. If you wish."

"I do, I do." Julietta laced her arm through Caroline's arm. "Please, lead the way."

TWENTY-TWO

Caroline and Julietta walked in silence along the banks of Arfiskeby. The Firefraught Lights hung in the sky; a dull throb of color filled the sky. They no longer shone with the same vibrance. Each time Caroline returned home, they appeared dimmer. Outside of her routes, Caroline often avoided Arfiskeby, worried her heart might break from all the changes. Tilda had long left her small town, and her brother and sister's lives continued undistributed by Caroline's death. The town itself remained suffocated by blight, with crops dying and more corucaish coming up shore, all while the Firefraught Lights dimmed. Whatever curse they believed Caroline carried hadn't gone away.

As Caroline expected.

She ended up releasing the souls of many men and women accused of witchcraft in town. Despite Priestess Abernathy, grayed with age and stress, saying that death did not solve the Constable's wrath, their fury continued to grow.

Yet, throughout the last decade, as Caroline explored the world, she realized... some things were indeed outside of the Constable's control. Sometimes, things just happened. The world wasn't always that complicated.

That was what Caroline told herself, at least.

Julietta stayed by Caroline's side as they watched over the water, shoulder-to-shoulder, her gaze cloudy. When she alas spoke, after hours of silence, her voice echoed, "Caroline... we must talk."

Caroline's stomach tumbled, "About?"

"I have not been truthful with you... and you are my dear friend... and I would hate to keep secrets." Julietta stroked back a strand of Caroline's hair.

Shivers worked their way up Caroline's back. "You do not owe me any sort of explanations, Julietta."

"But I do, Caroline," Julietta whispered, "You deserve to know."

"It does not matter, Julietta. Jiang... He is right. I never asked about you. It has always been about me." Caroline's voice split. "It has always been my problems... not yours."

"But I have not opened up to you either. I would rather embrace your problems on a good day and forget about my own." Julietta stepped towards the water. "Forgetting...that is my problem."

"I am confused." Caroline followed her friend.

Julietta sighed, "I am losing my memory, Caroline. It has been happening for decades...but I fear it is accelerating."

"You always seem sharp to me."

"But I am not. I only recall the past century. It started when I first became a Mist Keeper. I forgot my life and entered the world of the dead as a newborn child. I had to relearn how to be a Mist Keeper, but as I helped the dead...I slipped further. I cannot remember my apprentices; I only recall their names...and that they failed. I am slipping, and each day, I'm forgetting more." Julietta knelt down, the waves lapping against her knees as she stroked the water. "I paint what I remember, I paint the memories of others with the mist...but I cannot save my memories. Every day, I forget things. I knew Jiang didn't drink tea! But did I remember? No. Therefore, Caroline...I cannot be what you desire. For inevitably, I will forget."

Julietta lowered her head, her hair hanging over her face, eyes watering with tears. She appeared small, minuscule even, and Caroline did the only thing she could think of: she knelt beside her friend and embraced her tight.

Julietta's tears climbed to her throat, and she sobbed into Caroline's arms. It felt peculiar, being the comforter; usually, Caroline sought the attention and comfort. Should she pat Julietta on the back? Or whisper kindnesses and lies? How did she make someone feel... better?

She found a question in all the uncertainty. "Has Aelia tried to find a remedy? She has that healing magic."

"No, no, nothing works. The Mist Keepers cannot fix this. Tomás has tried as well, with his fancy mind manipulation abilities... but it is for naught." Julietta sighed. "Ningursu does not see any solution. He says comfort and support are all I need... but... I am scared. So very scared." Julietta tugged at the edge of her skirt. "I often wonder if I have any lost love out there... or family... or friends. I have searched, of course, but I do not even know if Julietta is my real name. It could have slipped from me when I died. While I trust Tomás told me the name he learned, my past alludes me. What if I lied to him when I met? What if they gave me the name I wanted? When your past changes every day, and your birth is moved forward with every forgotten memory, I cannot help but wonder... who am I?"

Caroline took Julietta's hands and held them close. She chose each word with care. The words danced over her lips. "You are Julietta of Spinoza, the Fourth Mist Keeper of the Council, and my dearest friend. You are kind. You listen. And I think, no matter what you forget, you will always want to help. Smiles are your blessings...and they will continue to shine in our Library."

Julietta squeezed Caroline's hand tight. Her smile ignited her face.

"And," Caroline continued, "I believe—as you would tell me—embrace the moment, for you are gorgeous, you are strong, and you will shine. Do not let one hindrance keep you from living."

"I have lived...or existed...a long time, Caroline. I am old enough to be your...well. That is too far back to count. You should not be ever so enthralled with me."

Caroline's face warmed, and she glanced at her feet. "Has it been so obvious?"

"Ever since we met." Julietta looked over her. "And I have found you spectacular as well. But I cannot promise a future."

"Well, I am not asking for the future. I am asking for a moment. For now."

"It would not be appropriate," Julietta whispered. "You are my friend and colleague. We cannot...we should not. But..."

"But?"

Julietta did not speak. Rather, she stepped forward and placed a hand on Caroline's cheek.

Caroline's entire body froze, like the permafrost out at sea.

Then, in the mere blink of an eye, Julietta stole a kiss.

The kiss warmed Caroline's body, and like the sun coming out at the start of summer, she melted like the ice. She closed her eyes, letting her heart hang between two beats, and her body relax.

The mist washed over them both, the kiss pulling them closer.

Then it ended, and when Caroline opened her eyes, Julietta had vanished.

TWENTY-THREE

Julietta left a linger of desire on Caroline's lips. For days, Caroline walked along in a haze of yearning, completing her routes but not living her moments. *Julietta feels the same way... but she is losing her memories. Will she forget me too?* Her thoughts continued along in these waves of uncertainty. She operated ambivalence, trying her best to determine what option made the most sense. Should she return to the Council and declare her love for Julietta? She had loved the woman longer than she had loved Tilda...but as Jiang said, what did Caroline really know? Julietta had only just opened her heart.

But for how long?

When would her heart succumb to this same fatal disease? When would she forget how to love, to hate...to be?

Caroline didn't see Julietta again for a fortnight. She would return after sixteen hours of releases, locking herself away in her office to ponder the options. To the Constable, love was sacred.

She loved Julietta. That much she understood.

And she would see Julietta through to the end of this...even if it meant the woman forgetting everything.

The decision came to her like a wave in the sea. It skimmed across the surface of her mind before hitting the rocks of pondering and dissonance. When it thrashed, then Caroline knew.

She wouldn't let Julietta fight this alone; friend, lover, or whatever they chose. She would fight by Julietta's side.

Caroline left her office in a hurry, not bothering to put on her shoes, as she hurried into the heart of the Library. Her heart carried her to the second floor, where Julietta's suite waited. Decorated canvases, with a miasma of memories painted upon them, guarded her hallway. Paint splattered the doorway while the carpet frayed at the edges beneath the doorframe.

As Caroline raised her hand to knock, the door opened.

Julietta stood before her like a portrait. Paint coated her skin and dress while the bright candle lights from her studio shone through into the Library. Caroline had only entered Julietta's room a few times before, but even from her spot, she could tell that the inside had changed. Half-painted canvases, paint stains, towers of leather-bound books, and piles of clothes filled the room. She couldn't even find Julietta's couch or the entrance to her private dwellings among the mess.

"Julietta, what has happened here?" Caroline asked, "Are you okay?"

"I have been...working." Julietta blinked a few times. Her eyes glistened with tears, and her bottom lip quivered. She continued, "Painting. I've been painting."

"What have you been painting?"

"My memories. What I could remember..." She motioned Caroline into the studio. Almost every painting stood half complete, except for one: the picture of Caroline, with half her face dripping, the other half pristine.

Caroline approached the picture.

"I see you so clear...remember everything about you so well. But when will I forget? When will my memories slip just like everything else here?" Julietta motioned to her incomplete paintings against the wall. One consisted of a young man playing the violin, but his face only comprised of a few smudges and sketch lines. Julietta approached it and stroked the canvas. "I once knew a young man...I've named him Milo. He used to play so many instruments. But I have no recollection of whether he was my brother, an apprentice, or something else. I cannot find those memories, Caroline. For days, I've been searching because...well, it does not matter."

Caroline glanced at the painting of herself. She swore it blinked. Then she turned to Julietta. "Why are you searching now? You seemed...content prior to our discussion."

"Because..." Julietta clenched her hand over the painting. "The other day made me realize...I am tired of walking through this afterlife in a fog. I want companionship and closeness, but I fear that...getting too close...I will lose everything. If I were to give myself to you, Caroline, I'd want to give you everything. But how can I if someday I might...forget?"

Caroline stepped forward, taking in Julietta's heartbreak with a single hand. She pressed it to Julietta's cheek. "I have spent the past fortnight thinking about what you mean to me, Julietta. And, I believe the Constable Gelida has given us many tasks in life—"

"You should know by now, Caroline, that I do not worship the Constable," Julietta said.

"Fine, then wherever you put your faith—"

"The Dueling Dragons of Spinoza."

"Pah, ridiculous." Caroline pulled back upon seeing Julietta's frown. "I apologize. I suppose it is no more ridiculous than a snow fairy goddess who rules over the permafrost."

"It is fine, Caroline. I have not prayed to the Dueling Dragons in many years. If they existed, why would they give me such a fate?"

"Well, we believe the Constable put each of us here for a reason, but that she can be a vengeful goddess if she pleases. So perhaps there is a reason for your memory loss, but..."

Caroline paused, letting the next few words melt over her tongue. She'd practiced this statement in some form for the past two weeks. She could say it now.

"But I believe my purpose now, not as a Mist Keeper but as a human, is to help you. We can try to find a cure. If anything...at least you will not be in this fight alone."

Julietta's eyes watered. "Caroline..."

"I am not yet jaded by the Council's nonchalance on the matter. I will help you as you have helped me. We can pull back the masks over your memories."

Julietta nodded, her tears still flowing, her body shaking. She only mustered two words: "Thank you."

Caroline's eyes pricked, but she sucked down the tears and embraced Julietta. Whatever came next, they would tackle with the force of a hundred horses running across the plains. Or perhaps an army of corucaish surrounding a small town, or the power of all the Mist Keepers that thrived in the world.

Together, in that moment, Caroline swore they could do anything.

TWENTY-FOUR

For years, Caroline and Julietta indeed tried to do anything and everything. They sorted through books to find Julietta's memories. They traveled the world, all while completing Caroline's dead routes, seeking seers and alchemists who might have a solution. They ventured to the lands in the south where herbs grew and to the deserts of Yilk to seek guidance from a wizard. Those with the sight of the Second World, the so-called Medii as Tilda described herself, eagerly awaited the Mist Keepers' arrival. But no one had a solution. Julietta had already tried most of what they offered, but most shrugged off her predicament as an ailment of the mist and outside of their purview.

None of the other Mist Keepers shared interest with them until one day when Caroline got a whiff of a powerful alchemist in the small nation-state of Merton. When she told Julietta, they prepared in excitement, only for Ningursu to call them into his office. It was the first time since Caroline's arrival that Ningursu called for her.

When Tomás brought them the notice, Caroline's stomach nearly poured out of her mouth. She gripped Julietta's hand as they headed up the stairs and ventured into the Head's office. Bookshelves towered over them while the haunted scent of mahogany filled the room. Ningursu, the Head of the Council, sat upon a pile of books. Despite only being a skull, his presence dominated the room. It cast a shadow of a skull on the wall, pulsing with black and yellow smoke.

When he opened his mouth to speak, the mist thickened. He boomed as soon as the door slammed shut. "Do not go to Merton. Do not seek their advice. They will not help you."

"But sir!" Caroline objected.

"We have done all we can do, as Julietta understands."

"We must keep trying—"

"Enough, Caroline." Ningursu closed his one white eye. "It is enough."

"For sard's sake—"

"ENOUGH!" Mist exploded from Ningursu's mouth and wrapped around Caroline. Like a chain, it wrapped around her body and tugged her close. She held her breath as his magic wrapped over her, and for a moment, Caroline swore she was no longer Caroline Walsh...but Ningursu himself.

Then the spell broke, and Caroline stumbled backwards into Julietta's arms. She stared at Ningursu, her mouth ajar. She'd never seen him lash out before, but now, the Head of the Council peered at her with the power of a God.

Ningursu did not flinch. "We have more important things to deal with, Caroline. The mist needs your guidance. Please, continue your work."

Caroline's throat tightened as she went to protest as if Ningursu's misty grip still took hold of her throat. She bowed her head in submission, only mouthing the words, "Yes, sir."

"Very good. You are dismissed." Ningursu's office door flew open behind her, and without another word, the mist dragged Caroline from the room.

Julietta followed her, eyes downcast, her blonde hair hiding her face. Her shoulders sagged, her lip quivered, but she said nothing.

Caroline immediately sat up once the door closed. "Hogwash!"

"Caroline! Do not curse!" Julietta exclaimed.

"I swear, I should march back in there and throw that consarn head against the wall!"

"Caroline!"

"He does not want us to succeed. Is that not obvious? That alchemist in Merton could surely help you, Julietta—"

"If Ningursu says they can't, then they can't. We have been searching for answers for a long while. I think...it is time to admit that my memory will one day be nothing more than a gasp of air." Julietta ran her fingers through the mist. "It is my curse, I suppose. Just as you were cursed to wear a mask."

"My mask is not a curse."

"But isn't it?"

"No! It has given me a chance to be me!"

"Caroline, my dear Caroline..." Julietta cupped her cheek. "*Who* is Caroline?"

"What are you talking about?"

"You are always focused on different goals, but what is your goal?"

"I want to help you because I love you, Julietta! That is my goal."

"But what if you cannot? What will you do with the hundreds of years to follow?"

Caroline didn't reply.

"My future is sealed, so I must do my best to prepare. But you have a life ahead of you. How long have you been a Mist Keeper now? Only a couple of decades. There is so much more to do...so why not live it, dear?"

Caroline wrung her hands. A knot tightened in her throat, and she directed her gaze towards the ground. Slowly, she spoke, keeping her voice steady, "Because I fear living it alone."

"You are not alone, dear."

"The Council does not count. Alojzy is amiss, Malaika is never here, Jiang is a twat, Tomás is pretentious, Aelia is shrewd, Ningursu is evasive, and you are...forgetting." Caroline could feel her mask slipping as emotions ran over her heart. "What am I supposed to do once you have forgotten me?"

Julietta took Caroline's hands. "There are more people in the world, dead and alive, who are there to be by your side, my dear. I love how you tried to help. I wanted to be helped as well. But we cannot keep searching in vain. Perhaps instead of investing so much in me, we can find those who can invest time in you. You shan't be alone. I promise."

TWENTY-FIVE

As the years passed, Julietta's memories continued to fade. Despite how she struggled, though, Julietta resolved to help Caroline find her family. Together, they wandered through the mist, searching for any sign of familiar faces and welcoming arms.

They found the soul of Caroline's father wandering along the coast of Arfiskeby, not far from where they buried his body. Based on his own account, Alojzy released him years ago, but the man had not moved on, still waiting for his wife to return home from the sea. Caroline greeted him like a distant relative. They did not embrace, nor did they even smile. Her father hadn't fathered her in his last years, and she had abandoned him in a time of crisis. They acknowledged each other with a silent nod, staring out at the melting permafrost. The curse of the corucaish marked their lives, left to rot in the arms of the melting sea. Yet even after they had both passed, the corucaish's curse remained.

The world would succumb to whatever Constable Gelida had planned.

As the sun fell, Caroline and her father split, going their separate ways. Caroline did not seek him out again for many years; he had not cradled her close, nor did she run to his arms. But he had found peace, and that much Caroline respected.

Caroline continued to spend her years conducting releases. Despite Julietta's insistence that Caroline should build a camaraderie with the dead, she kept her head bowed. There was no reason to interact in Caroline's eyes. Their world acted much different from her world... and they only overlapped because of death.

Some days, Julietta joined her on the routes, but most days, Caroline went alone. With every passing week, Julietta grew more distant. She forgot important dates and tasks. Other days, Caroline just found her staring at the wall, holding a paintbrush, her eyes lost in thought. Even on the days when she appeared more present, she spoke little, wandering along Caroline's side with her arm looped through hers, mouth pursed in a frown.

Loneliness became Caroline's companion. Even when her brother and sister both passed away, and she released their souls, they reunited with both happiness and horror. Her brother and sister rejoiced, of course, upon seeing her but backed away, fearful of Caroline's new role. Could she be a witch? A minion of the Constable's curse? Or was she still their sister?

Even if they came to accept her as their sister, any time they saw each other came with the same distance they had during their lives. After all, William and Victoria both lived a full life, aged into their years, with children and grandchildren to mark the path.

Caroline stood only in the mist, watching the lives of others pass before her, with no one by her side.

Except for Julietta.

Fading...

Fading...

And fading away...

It grew worse as the days passed. Caroline eagerly awaited Julietta's knock on her door each morning. Yet, with the passing of time, Julietta's consistency faded. She started knocking at odd hours or forgetting altogether. First, the knocks started every other day, then once a week, and eventually, Caroline had to knock on her friend's door instead.

With the heaviness mounting that Julietta may soon forget everything, even Caroline toyed with the idea of going against Ningursu and seeking the alchemist in Merton. Yet, whenever the idea crossed her mind, it was as if the mist suffocated her all over again. She could go to Merton and watch the alchemist from afar, but if she dared to step forward and reveal herself, if she dared even attempt the idea, then Ningursu's wrath remained.

There was nothing she could do for her dearest friend.

Except knock on her door.

Caroline took that up as her job. Each day, she checked on Julietta. Sometimes, Julietta turned from her paintings with a smile, but other days, she kept her gaze focused, brow furrowed, as she tried to recall the memory to paint out of the mist. There came days when Julietta walked with Caroline, just as they'd done in their romance and smiles. But others came as well when Julietta never left her room nor acknowledged Caroline at all.

Everything changed about Julietta in subtle waves. First, her speech grew softer, kissing the air in song. Then she stopped combing her hair. Paint covered her clothes and skin, and unless coerced by someone, she failed to bathe for days. Caroline, as well as the others, had to remind her to eat. Every now and again, she even got lost in the Library.

But Caroline refused to let Julietta slip.

Not yet.

But no matter what she did, whether she created masks to make Julietta laugh or reminded Julietta of her personal history, it was for naught.

Julietta's mind continued to fade like the mist.

TWENTY-SIX

Caroline's one-hundredth anniversary of becoming a Mist Keeper came with dull congratulatory remarks from most of the Council. Alojzy applauded her success, while the others merely sent kind smiles in her direction. It should have been a momentous occasion, a celebration of sorts, but only one thing hung in Caroline's heart: Julietta.

In the last month, she'd seen her friend maybe three times. Aelia and Tomás informed Caroline that Julietta had fallen ill, and her memories slipped faster by the minute. Constantly busy with her care, they never allowed Caroline to enter.

She slipped into the infirmary a few times to visit Julietta. Her friend remained on the bed, unaware of Caroline's presence. Caroline would whisper her name, take her hand, and pray to the Constable for things to change. What could she do but wait? Before her, Julietta withered... and Caroline could only mask her own emotions with a faux face.

As always, alone.

She continued, alone.

Soon after her one-hundredth anniversary, Tomás approached Caroline as she wandered the Library shelves. Tomás emerged from between the shelves like a ghost. He placed a hand on her shoulder.

Caroline jumped, spinning around to whack Tomás with the back of her hand. "What are you doing!?!"

"Caroline! Please!" Tomás pressed a hand to his cheek. "I needed your attention."

"You could have spoken my name."

"Perhaps." Tomás blinked a few times, squinting, "I wanted to talk to you."

"What about?"

"Julietta."

Caroline's stomach fell. "What about her?"

"Well, the good news is she is doing better." Tomás sat in a chair, crossing his legs and leaning back to stare at the ceiling.

"And the bad news?" Caroline prodded.

"Her memory is...scrambled. That is the best word for it. I took a deep dive into her mind for a better look. It is like a fallen forest, with only a skeleton of trees standing. Those are her remaining memories, and if she touches the right one, she remembers it. But mostly, she is wandering over fallen trees, trying her best to understand the pieces of bark like a newborn child. She understands some of it, but otherwise, her mind is like... a pasture of farmland."

"What? Why do you speak in such riddles?"

"Caroline," Tomás said, "she has forgotten almost everything at this point. I am sorry."

Caroline stopped herself from crying out, "But...she has to remember. She cannot forget...everything. Can she not relearn those memories? Rebuild them?"

Tomás rubbed the bridge of his nose and said, "I do not know. She has had bouts like this in the past, where she forgets some of what happened, but never to this extent. She never recuperated those memory gaps. I think this will be her new normal. Her reality will be fractions of the past melding with the now; she will be a ghost, but she will survive."

Caroline stumbled backwards, her body trembling, "No...she has to remember. She must..."

"Caroline."

"She must!"

Before Tomás called out again, Caroline darted off into the shelves and towards the stairwell. She jumped over every other step, her heart thudding, only to be masked out by her feet. At the top of the stairs, she nearly toppled into Jiang, who threw a glower in her direction but no snide remarks. She didn't bother apologizing, racing to Julietta's door and throwing it open without knocking.

Julietta stood by one of her canvases, paintbrush in hand. She didn't turn as Caroline entered.

"Julietta?" Caroline called out. Her friend didn't turn still. She continuously brushed the same spot on the canvas with purple, but nothing else took shape.

Caroline approached her slowly, calling out her name a few more times. On the last one, Julietta finally turned.

A smile broke open on her lips, her eyes alight. "Ah! Milo! It is so good to see you!"

Caroline's stomach fell. "Milo?"

"That's your name, isn't it? Come, Milo, come sit. I am working on my newest painting. You can watch; yes, you can. Right, Milo? Please sit."

"Julietta...I am not Milo. I am Caroline."

"Caroline? No. No. That's not right..." She turned back to the canvas. "That can't be right."

Biting back her sorrow, Caroline stepped back from her friend. Silent.

Unsure.

Waiting.

Julietta turned back to her canvas, humming an off-beat tune.

No words.

No acknowledgment.

Alone.

Once certain Julietta had forgotten her presence, Caroline stepped out of the room and let the mask melt from her face with her tears.

TWENTY-SEVEN

Caroline wandered. She conducted her releases with few breaks, with no connection to any of the souls she released. Each one became nothing more than a checkmark; whether she released a giant from Yilk or a child from Janis, all remained the same.

Nothing was unique.

All mist.

The illusions of grandeur and success faded.

She was nothing but a ghost, given a duty and left alone.

A hundred years of her life had gone in a blink of an eye; she still remembered her mother's death as clear as anything and Tilda's lips like a blossoming rose. Her time with the Council had passed like a gasp of air.

And now, without Julietta, she wore the mask of oblivion. Caroline had one goal: free souls, don't grow attached, and continue with her journey.

Not that the journey took her anywhere at all.

Suns rose and set. She no longer wore her mask. If she had ever been the woman in black with the painted red lips, she died with Julietta's memories.

Alone.

As always.

Alone.

Her wandering always brought her home to Arfiskeby. Whenever she let the mist take hold of her, it guided her to the coastline of her old home. In the hundred years since her death, the permafrost had thawed, leaving a thin glow against the horizon, where Helvidim waited. Above, the Firefraught Lights throbbed, their colors dull and lackluster.

As if the Constable Gelida herself looked upon Caroline in shame.

Whenever Caroline realized she had returned home, she left as soon as possible, disappearing again into the mist to continue her endless cycle of releases.

Only to come back again to Arfiskeby.

The sixth time it happened, Caroline finally snapped, glowering at her own two feet.

"Consarn it! How dare you bring me back here! I do not want to be here! Let me just be in peace!" She kicked one of her shoes into the water. No one, alive or dead, saw her, the mist acting like a cloak from the living. She continued to shriek in frustration. Why did she keep coming back? What did it matter?

The sea always calls me back... Caroline approached the edge of the water to retrieve her shoe. She let the water stroke her fingertips, then recede. Unlike her days as a child, this water did not shimmer; rather, it sat dark beneath the dim Firefraught Lights. Was the curse of the corucaish still lingering? Or something else, far beyond the Constable Gelida's reign?

What have I done to my homeland? Caroline stared towards the pier. If she never found the corucaish, would the sea still glimmer? Would the Firefraught Lights still shine?

Would her mother have returned home?

"Mama... what happened?" Caroline stepped into the water. "I never found you, Mama."

She stared at her hands. Calloused from her early life of working ropes, in death, they never disappeared. She might not have sailed for years, but it ran through her blood, with the sea calling her name.

As a child, Caroline made a promise to her brother.

I will find her... and I will be the best.

She had been the best.

The best fisher.

The best apprentice.

The best friend.

And now, she would finally become the best daughter.

TWENTY-EIGHT

With her newfound rejuvenation, Caroline returned to the Library for the first time in months. Tomás tried to interrogate her, but she locked herself away to focus on the task at hand. She would have to get a boat and navigate to Helvidim, all while trusting her instincts as a Mist Keeper to guide the way to her mother's lost soul.

She planned her escape for weeks, keeping to her routine, before finally meeting up in the tunnels with Malaika, the elusive Mist Keeper with a knack for cartography. Caroline hadn't spent a lot of time with Malaika, truthfully. She had been Jiang's apprentice but acted as a foil to his argumentative nature. Rather than moping around the Library, Malaika traveled the world. She used different contraptions to navigate the lands:

boats with churning gears, horses cloaked in mist, and even a floating contraption guided by hot air.

So, when Caroline came to her, Malaika obliged with a wide smile and smacked a hand on Caroline's back. Despite her small stature, Malaika's strength took Caroline by surprise, and she stumbled forward a few steps.

"Of course, I can get ya that boat. Strong hull and everything. Leave it to me." Malaika replied.

Caroline rubbed her shoulder. "Thank you. And a map... I need a map of the permafrost."

"I'll see what I can do. And if you need a crew, I got a whole group of lasses who might want to help—"

"I must do this alone."

Malaika didn't inquire further but promised Caroline that she'd find a boat within a fortnight. Caroline thanked her before returning to her routes, focusing on the task ahead.

In childhood, her studies told her that the permafrost expanded further than the eyes could see, reaching out across the edges of the world. With it melting, Caroline couldn't be sure how long it would take to navigate. Before the curse of the corucaish, her mother told her they spent months navigating the permafrost and still hadn't discovered it all.

Now Caroline was determined to navigate the whole thing, especially if it meant finding her mother.

I will be the best. She kept reciting as she released each soul. *I will be successful.*

The promise guided her movements, and as she came back to the Library each day, she wore that goal imprinted on her heart. Malaika created a map that Caroline spent days memorizing, watching as the mist repositioned the permafrost each day. It no longer sat permanently against the water but shifted like a moving glacier. The world was changing... and fast.

But Caroline didn't let it deter her.

A week before setting off on her voyage, Caroline pulled on her black cloak and voyaged upstairs to Ningursu's office. Aelia, Tomás, and Alojzy watched her from different corners of the Library, but no one said a word. Caroline let them stare. She had grown used to it; she had abandoned her mask of beauty, no longer searching to impress a beautiful woman with white hair, and walked forward with the honest but determined face of a monster.

And when she knocked on Ningursu's door, she wore that face with pride.

Instead, she strode forward, her voice level.

"Caroline." Ningursu sat on his desk, as per usual. He held the room in his stare, the mist twirling around him without stopping. Caroline admired him, to an extent; while he wore the determination of a God, he also kept thriving... despite his predicament. He didn't let his missing body deter him.

Caroline knelt before his desk. "Ningursu, sir, I have a request."

"You would like to take a sabbatical, correct?" Ningursu asked without flinching.

"Well, yes. That is what I was going to ask."

"It is granted. You have one month."

"Oh? Really?" Caroline stumbled back from Ningursu. She had prepared a speech to convince Ningursu; now all of that flew out of her mind as her mouth hung ajar.

Ningursu continued, "You have been the most productive Mist Keeper in your hundred years of service. We have not had someone so efficient, and we can only hope that your future apprentice will live up to these expectations. You can rest easy for the next month. The Council shall thrive without you."

"Thank you, sir." Caroline rose, "Really. I promise I will be back in a month... and I will continue to be the best I can be."

"I am sure of that, Caroline. Good luck finding your mother."

"Thank you," Caroline whispered one last time, then with a swish of her black cloak and the click of her heels, she headed out the door to exit the Library.

TWENTY-NINE

Malaika found Caroline a boat with a hull composed of reinforced steel. Small enough for her to sail on her own, Caroline thanked Malaika with a payment of a carved fishing rod she found abandoned in a home outside Arfiskeby. They didn't stop to chat, and Caroline boarded her ship, once more wrapped in her memories of sailing in her teenage years. She played the part of all the sailors, wearing their faces as masks, bringing in the ropes, manning the navigation, and casting the nets out to sea for food.

The sea, with an open view of the Firefraught Lights, cast a net of peace and tranquility over her. Salt whisked through the air, riding on freezing winds and lashing against Caroline's cheek. She breathed each whiff, leaning against the edge of the railing, watching as the mist-laden whales breached the surface in the distance. Around them, gulls flew, and a few salmon fish bounced around in the waves.

As night descended, the Firefraught Lights glowed a dim green. With it, the further Caroline traveled into the arms of the permafrost, the more the landscape pulsed with life, death, and mist. In the darkest hours of night, the corucaish emerged, glowing silver and riding on the currents of the past. Caroline watched them in awe. Away from her home, they moved like beasts, but they also rose like the sun. As they moved, streams of silver followed, reminiscent of the elixirs and potions Tilda used many years ago.

Caroline's heart sank. She hadn't sought Tilda, nor had she found her soul. Perhaps she still lived on, old and wise, telling futures and helping others reach their own true selves.

One day, they would see each other again.

When? Caroline didn't know.

Tilda probably already knew.

Caroline continued watching the permafrost, listening as her hull cracked open the ice and as the wind blew through the air. It caught her hair, casting masks over her face with each puff of mist. Caroline followed each mask, letting them solidify on her face, replacing her blotched skin with faces of others: a man who drowned in a storm, a child who fell overboard, and a young woman eaten by a fish. Each death bore a familiar tale, and Caroline reached out over the sea to release each soul, one at a time.

One.

Two.

Three.

And more.

Yet despite each soul, none beckoned her like her mother. She did not find her mother's face on her skin.

She found only strangers.

But Caroline refused to give up, especially after all this time. She owed her father, her siblings, and herself to find her mother.

So, she continued along, counting the days by the colors of the Firefraught Lights. When they rose with a twinge of red, it meant another day had passed. When they set with a gasp of blue, it meant night had fallen. In that time, she recanted to herself all the souls she helped release and all the leagues she had hence traveled.

When souls did not call for her, when voices did not cry, she fished. She caught her meals, she diluted her water, and she survived alone for a fortnight. At first, she caught only salmon and other common fish.

But soon, corucaish filled her lines.

She set them free without a thought, praying their curse might leave her alone.

Yet the corucaish did not abandon Caroline. She tried to shoo them off, but with each stroke of her paddle or tossing of net, the fish kept their resolve. Even when she ignored them, they remained, and over time, an army of the silver fish gathered at the base of her hull. They jumped through the air, their silver eyes wide with glee, riding in the arms of the mist. Each time they jumped, the Firefraught Lights coated their skin in an incandescent rainbow of color.

They moved like shooting stars across the water.

Like the stars, they said, the Constable Gelida rose to bless the world by her hand.

Perhaps they are not a curse at all. Caroline lowered her fingers to the water one evening. The corucaish gathered at her fingers. They spun in a circle, then lowered beneath her ship as if bowing to her.

It seems they want to help.

The next time the Firefraught Lights turned green, Caroline followed the corucaish through the permafrost, letting them serve as her guide. The mist followed them as well, lassoed in awe by the glistening beasts. Each time they jumped, Caroline's face changed, telling the tale of a different person sent to death by the wrath of the freezing ocean.

And she continued releasing souls until she met the darkest corners of the world, where the permafrost stopped her boat in its tracks. The only light came from a single star hanging above her and the shimmering skins of the corucaish. Caroline stared out, holding her breath.

Her face shifted again.

There, at the edge of the world, she finally found the answer to her prayers.

THIRTY

Caroline felt her mother's soul before the mask appeared. It called for her, a gentle hum reminiscent of the lullabies her mother sang at night. Touch reaffirmed her identity: cheeks hardened by years at sea, chapped lips from the taste of salt, and hair always knotted by days of wind. Caroline didn't need to see her mother's face to know she bore it as a mask.

"Take me to her," Caroline spoke into the dark sky. "I know she is here."

The mist raised around her, and with it, she let the corucaish guide her into the darkness of the permafrost. She wore the darkness like a cloak, imagining herself as the confident, beautiful woman in black from Tilda's vision. Here she was in her element.

She could move like a shadow, act like a Mist Keeper, and be a predator.

And she would succeed.

The further she got along the edge of the world, the less the corucaish glimmered. *Mama, what took you out this far?* Caroline gripped the edge of her boat as the water carried her along the arms of the mist. With each passing minute, her mask grew more pronounced. She bore her mother's face, and like all the souls before, she would wear it until arriving at the final resting place.

She brought her boat to a halt as the mask solidified. The mist dropped away from her just as she reached an island of ice. Rocks lay scattered about it while ice tortoises slept on the beach, their shells glistening like diamonds. The snow roared, casting a wall of white before her. Each snowflake latched onto the wool of her cloak, transforming her into a painting of the sky.

Caroline pushed forward as the mist thickened. Her mask tugged her forward, and with her heart full and throat tight, she walked along the coastline. A fixture of steel and wood waited for her, untouched by the weather and storm.

My mother's boat. She approached the hull, its steel rusted by the weather. Upon the bow, her ship's name glistened still: *Vicarlliam*. Caroline still remembered when her mother named the ship. She took each of her children's names and mashed them together in a nonsense word. She laughed to herself. *It is still quite absurd.* She traced the words, then stepped inside the bones of the ship.

The mist vanished as she entered. A boneyard welcomed her. Amid the bones, a large white bear slept, huddled with cubs. Caroline used a cloak of mist to hide from the bear and wandered through the carcasses of seals, tortoises, and foxes.

Beyond where the bear slept lay three preserved human bodies. Ice coated their blue skin, and their hair hung like icicles. She recognized the first two men from her mother's ship, never to return home, lost at sea. Their souls vanquished their bodies with a mere touch, and as per usual, seeped into the mist.

Bile rose in Caroline's throat as she approached the last body. After one hundred years, she had grown numb to the bodies piling around her. She trained her sense not to falter, imaging the scent of the sea whenever she approached a body laced with rot. Death became salt, sifting over the sandy shores, rising against the glaciers in the distance, and waving in the breeze.

But staring at the body of her mother, frozen by time and captured by snow, all that training disappeared. She withered to her knees like a child and brushed back her mother's hair. As tears bubbled in her eyes, she lowered her lips to her mother's forehead and released her with a kiss.

THIRTY-ONE

Katherine Walsh emerged in a funnel of mist, her soul pulsing in and out like a weak heartbeat. Caroline stepped back as her mother blinked a few times. Her soul mimicked her body before death, a tall, proud woman with sleek black hair and weather-worn skin. Her blue eyes copied Caroline's eyes, wide with wonder, while her thin lips pulled back in a gentle smile.

"Caroline... is that you?" Katherine asked.

"It is me, Mama. I came to find you." Caroline choked.

"You found me..."

"Yes, I found you."

"But... this is not home... this is past the permafrost in the Constable Gelida's land..." Her mother scanned

Caroline with reticence, "This must have taken many years to find."

"More than one hundred, Mama."

"One hundred years... but how? You are so young."

"I have so much to tell you. It is... long and complicated. But I have done so much, Mama."

"Then please, tell me, Caroline."

"Do you not wish to rest first?"

"I have rested in my nightmares. Please, talk to me now."

"Very well."

Sitting in the snow, Caroline told her mother everything. She detailed the years after her mother disappeared, her journey as a fisher, the curse of the corucaish, as well as her own transformation into a Mist Keeper. She skimmed quickly over her romances with Tilda and Julietta, avoiding the details that left her blushing, and her years of diving deep into her work. Her mother didn't speak, nodding to the story, just as she used to when Caroline was a child.

"And that led me here..." Caroline finished, staring out from the hull of the broken ship towards the sea. "I had to find you."

Her mother said nothing at first, following Caroline's gaze out to sea. The silence held the air in its embrace before finally being broken with a single sigh.

"Oh, Caroline."

"What?"

"You have always been a determined child...but you get lost in the sea."

"I do not understand."

"Ever since you were a little girl, Caroline, you always promised to do *things*... and those became your goals. I remember you and Victoria once competed in who could grow their hair the longest. Despite how badly your hair matted and despite how it reached your ankles, even after Victoria cut her hair, you refused until you had a new fixation. Next, you wanted to be as strong as the boys in town, so you practiced carrying bags of goods to and from the pier until you broke an arm. Now, you have spent one hundred years searching for me. It is admirable, but... for sard's sake, Caroline..." Her mother placed a hand on Caroline's cheek. "You need to rest."

"But I found you—" Caroline started to say.

"Yes. But now what?"

Caroline laughed to herself, "I will go on and be a Mist Keeper."

"Until you need an apprentice?"

"And then I will be their teacher."

"But will you be ready to be their teacher, Caroline?"

"Pardon?"

Her mother brushed back Caroline's hair, "You cannot teach if you have not learned."

"I know how to be a Mist Keeper! Consarn it, Mama, I found you!"

"Yes, but I told you this as a child, Caroline. It is not enough to be the best. You must also learn how to be *you*. And you have time to discover yourself. By the sounds of it, you have an eternity. Do not cling to goals. Sometimes, let go and live."

Caroline didn't know what to say. Since her mother vanished, she held onto this promise. *What will you do now?* The words echoed. What would she do? What did the others *do*? Julietta painted, but she also forgot. Jiang brewed, but he also mulled and pouted. Tomás read both hearts and minds. Malaika explored with a laugh on her lips. Caroline had fishing, but what else?

What more could she be but a Mist Keeper?

Her mother interjected Caroline's thoughts, stepping forward as she stared out at the water. "I never told you why I fish, did I?"

"I always assumed it was because you dreamt of finding the greatest catch and securing our family," Caroline replied.

"Perhaps that was the goal when I first stepped onboard a ship. But...as I grew, the sea became my peace. Yes, it killed me in the end, but I do not blame the sea or the corucaish or the Constable Gelida. The storms come, as they do, and they whisked me away into the arms of the permafrost. That seemed like a poetic end for me, taken by the water I always loved and helped me realize my true self." Her mother ran her fingers over the sand. "I was a fisher, but I also loved sunsets, my husband, and my children. I died without finishing my tale of the sea, but at least my legacy lives on with my children. But it is not just my legacy anymore... it is yours as well. So, Caroline, it is time to build your legacy. But make it *your* legacy. Not mine. Not the Mist Keepers. *Yours.*"

Caroline turned away and crossed her arms. She glowered out at the field of bones behind her. The white bear amongst them stirred, rolling onto her side so the cubs could nurse. In peace, the creature slept, content with its role in the ever-changing landscape of the world.

"I love you so much, Caroline. I spent all these past years in constant darkness, in Hell as you so call it, and I clung to the memory of you, of Victoria, and of William. I dreamt of your futures, but I never imagined this for you. But now, I hope now you can find the future you so desire."

Caroline twiddled her thumbs and clenched her jaw. Her voice cracked. "Consarn it, Mama. Can you not just be happy with my success?"

"I am so happy and so grateful, Caroline. And so, so proud of you. But," her mother caught a strand of Caroline's hair and tucked it behind her ear, "I want you to be happy. Not an illusion of happiness... but pure happiness. A type of happiness you can wear with pride."

Caroline touched her own cheek, recalling the mask she used to wear during her years enthralled with Julietta. That mask, the beauty dominated by a woman with red lips, marked her happiest years. It marked years full of confidence and love. It melted with Julietta's memory, and she never thought she would harness it again.

But she could try.

And she would.

"I shall try, Mama," Caroline said. "I promise."

THIRTY-TWO

Caroline sailed through the permafrost with her mother for three days. Her mother taught her more about the sea while detailing parts of her life and adventures Caroline had never been told. Mother and daughter, sailing across the sea, fishing together in death; this had been Caroline's dream since childhood. Now, what could she dream of next?

Her mother couldn't give her the answer; only she could determine it herself.

As she docked her boat along the coastal pier of her hometown, she realized their voyage had at last ended. Her mother smiled at her, placed a hand on her cheek, then, with a single wisp of mist, vanished.

Someday, perhaps, Caroline might see her again, as she had seen her father, sister, and brother. But her mother now had a place within the mist to dance with the Constable Gelida and be at peace that she had lived.

With her heart heavy and body tired, Caroline wandered back to the Library, once again alone. The tunnels greeted her like an old friend, and upon approaching the towering doors of the Library, they welcomed her with an emotionless embrace.

She didn't seek anyone as she entered the Library. Jiang glanced at her first from his perch on the second-floor balcony, and as she walked to her suite, he mimicked her walk from above, a smirk on his face. If he spoke, she did not hear.

She had no reason to see Ningursu. He probably already heard she had returned to the Library. He had eyes, ears, and understanding of everything. More likely, he had already heard of the events at sea.

Much to Caroline's surprise, dust did not cover her suite after a month of absence. In fact, everything remained pristine, as if stuck in ice. She dragged her finger along the empty bookshelf, then glanced around her suite. The room itself, despite its elegance and prestige, bore no identifying marks but for the couple fishing nets and the mural of the sea painted on the wall. Unlike Julietta's studio or Ningursu's cluttered office, this could have belonged to anyone.

She trailed into her bedroom, where the bed remained unkempt, a single cloak hanging off the edge. Caroline stroked the material, then stripped off her sea-worn clothing and kicked it to the side. After pulling out a long chemise, she stared at herself in the mirror. She had yet to reclaim her face, once again peering back at a blotched monster.

While poking her skin a couple times, she imagined herself again as the woman in black, with red-painted lips, commanding attention. What did that woman want in life? There was no answer to that question. In fact, in some ways, it caused bubbles of excitement to rise in Caroline's stomach.

She didn't have to be controlled by one goal. As her mother said, she had an eternity to see and learn everything.

The possibilities were endless, and with them, a smile formed on her lips. Light filled her eyes. Mist twirled.

And once again, her confidence shone through, replacing her blotched, spongy face with a new mask.

This mask didn't change her imperfection. In the right light, she could still make out her black and blue marks. But with the mask, she might just become who she wanted.

She forced a smile, only for it to drop when a knock echoed through her suite.

"One moment, please!" she called. Upon pulling on a dark red overdress, she raced to the door.

Julietta stood on the other side, holding a cup of tea in her hands. She beamed, "Ah! Caroline!"

"You... know my name?" Caroline stared.

"Of course I do, silly. What kind of question is that?"

"Well—"

"How were your routes today? Do you need any help? I know being new to the Council is cumbersome."

"Julietta, I have been a part of this for over a hundred years."

"Oh no, that cannot be right. You only joined last week!" Julietta thrust the cup of tea into Caroline's hands. "Drink. You look pale."

Caroline took the cup as Julietta waltzed into the room, running her fingers along a shelf. She removed a cloth from her dress and began polishing it, humming to herself.

Despite everything, she is so carefree and content. Caroline brought the cup to her lip, watching her old beloved dust the shelf with her paint-covered fingertips.

Julietta stopped at the bare shelf. "You have no books, dear."

"I do not really read."

"Oh, well, here!" Julietta reached into the pocket of her dress. Out she pulled a leather-bound book, stained by paint, with pages crumpled and the spine cracked. "I found this. It's a book... you might like it, dear."

Caroline placed her cup down and took the book. The title, inscribed in old Spinozan, read: *The Woman's Muse by Julietta du Ville Ciel.*

She skimmed over the first few pages. This old story bled through her fingers, recanting a painter pursuing a romance with a prince in a tower. After the beginning, Caroline could already feel her heart warm and face flush. The descriptions were so vivid and lovely they would keep her awake late into the night.

When Caroline finally closed the book, Julietta stared at her with a smile. She returned it before glancing again at the title. "Julietta du Ville Ciel..." she whispered. "Did you write this?"

"Me? No. No. Who's to say?" Julietta smiled, "It is a lovely story, though, dear. Read it. I promise you will love it."

"Oh, well, thank you then." Caroline placed the book on the table, stealing one last glance at the cover.

Julietta's grin did not falter as she placed her kerchief back in her pocket before sitting on the couch. Despite everything, she still was the same woman Caroline knew.

Still the same woman she loved.

Still the same woman who sat by the sea with her.

Caroline approached her dearest friend, "Julietta?"

"Yes, Caroline?" Her eyes twinkled.

"Would you like to go fishing with me today?"

"Fishing? I do not know if I have fished before."

"If you dislike it, you can always paint the sea."

"Paint the sea... yes... yes, that I'd like." Julietta grinned. "I shall go get my painting supplies now!"

"I will come get you from your room soon."

Julietta clapped, then rushed out of the room like a child. Caroline watched her leave, her heart full. Once the door shut, Caroline once again retired to her bedroom to retrieve her cloak. As she pulled a clean one out of her closet, she paused by the mirror and touched her pale, bare lips.

I can choose my destiny. The world is at my fingertips.

She reached into her drawers and pulled out red lip paint.

And for the first time, she painted her lips red.

WANT TO SEE MORE CAROLINE?

You can find her in
THE LIFE & DEATH CYCLE

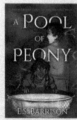
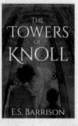

The Story Collector's Almanac

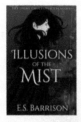  

Also by E.S. Barrison...

Tales from the Effluvium
Speak Easy

The Unsought Fairytale Collection
Tuppence
Focaccia

Author's Note

Thank you so much for taking the time to read *Illusions of the Mist*.

If you enjoyed this book, I would appreciate it if you could:

Review this book. Reviews are a great help to an author. If you enjoyed this book, please consider leaving a review on Amazon or Goodreads.

Tell Others. When you share this book with others on social media, you're allowing others to discover this story. Word-of-mouth is one of the best sources of marketing for an author.

Connect with me. If you want to find out about my upcoming releases, stop by my website at www.esbarrison-author.com or connect with me on social media.

Thank you!

E.S. Barrison

ACKNOWLEDGMENTS

To all the following, my thanks, for your support, friendship, and kindness throughout this process:

First to Kimmi & Nicky, all those years we discussed Caroline came together in this story. It might not be the same character we met when we were thirteen, but the influences are there.

To Moira, my cover artist, for coming up with such a unique concept for the cover.

To Charlie, my editor, for helping me refine Caroline and bring her to life in this tale.

To Matthew, for giving me feedback and actually putting up with my antics

And finally, to my readers, I am so glad you love Caroline as much as me.

Without all of your support, this story would not have been possible.

About the Author

E.S. Barrison has been writing and creating stories for as long as she can remember. After graduating from the University of Florida, she has spent the past few years wrangling her experiences to compose unique worlds with diverse characters. Currently, E.S. lives in Orlando, Florida with her family.

http://www.esbarrison-author.com

Lightning Source UK Ltd.
Milton Keynes UK
UKHW020806260522
403565UK00011B/835